SINFUL DESIRES

ELITE HEIRS OF MANHATTAN BOOK 3

MISSY WALKER

Copyright © 2024 by Missy Walker

All rights reserved.

No part of this publication may be reproduced, distributed or transmitted in any form or by any means, including by any electronic or mechanical means, including photocopying, recording or information storage and retrieval systems, without prior written consent from the author, except for the use of brief quotations in a book review.

Cover Design: Missy Walker

Editor: Swish Design & Editing

*To Clem,
let's hope reading another one of my books doesn't get you pregnant again!*

Elite *Men* Of Manhattan and Elite *Heirs* of Manhattan Family Tree

BARRETT BLACK & LOURDE DIAMOND
FORBIDDEN LUST #1
FORBIDDEN LOVE #2

- COLTON BLACK
- SIENNA BLACK

CONNOR DIAMOND & PEPPER LITTLE
LOST LOVE #3

- LUCIAN DIAMOND

ARI GOLDSMITH & OLIVIA WILLOWS
MISSING LOVE #4

- ROSE GOLDSMITH
- NOAH GOLDSMITH

MAGNUS MILLER & EVELYN BLACK
GUARDED LOVE #5

- ARIA MILLER
- VALENTINA MILLER
- MILES YOUNG

SEDUCTIVE HEARTS #1
COLTON AND ROSE

SWEET SURRENDER #2
NOAH AND SIENNA

SINFUL DESIRES #3
ARIA AND MILES

1

ARIA

"*Sorry about that, sis.*"

Four words with the power to take everything I thought I knew and turn it upside down.

From a complete stranger.

Thoughts of my parents' happy marriage and my secure family hit me all at once. So many of my friends came from miserably broken homes and hardly knew their parents. I used to think we were better than them. Looking back, it's not something I was proud of.

Only the sharp pain in my bottom lip alerted me to the fact that I was chewing the hell out of it, gazing out the window of the SoHo restaurant where my sister was supposed to meet me for lunch. She would be as shocked as I was when I confessed everything that went down earlier when I learned exactly how a deer feels when headlights bear down on them.

The only thing I couldn't convey was how he'd made me feel for weeks. Showing up in random places. The spin class where he'd stared daggers at me until I couldn't stand the thought of showing my face. Standing behind me in Starbucks. Hanging around outside the restaurant where Valentina and I ate dinner a week ago. It had gotten to the point where I looked for him wherever I went.

He hadn't said a word until today, but there hadn't been a need to. His intense energy spoke volumes until he'd decided to stop playing around and finally introduce himself as a member of my family.

"My name is Miles." He offered a charming grin while his eyes—green flecked with gold and apparently blessed with the ability to stare through me—darted over my face, searching for my reaction to his little announcement. It made my skin crawl the way he observed me like a predator anticipating his prey's first move.

What was I thinking? He was nobody. A creep with an accent. "I don't care what your name is, and I don't care what scam you're trying to pull." I snatched my matcha latte from him, which, for some reason, made him laugh like there was something funny about that. "And if you think you're the first person ever to claim you came from one of my dad's swimmers, think again. I'm not impressed."

"So distrusting," he murmured. His accent would've been a serious turn-on if the rest of him wasn't so repulsive. The sensual mouth now curved in a knowing grin. The laughter in his eyes. He scrubbed a hand over his head, raking his fingers through short, dirty blond curls that were just a little too long. They gave him sort of a roguish look.

"Whatever you say." I wasn't about to give him another moment of my time. There I was, worrying about him being a dangerous stalker when really he was nothing but a pathetic jerk with a scam in mind. Why he'd spent weeks intimidating me was anybody's guess.

"Why don't you ask your father?" he called out to my back. I

turned away, determined to forget he existed. "Ask him about Leila."

I paused my retreat, turning slowly to find him sneering down at me. What was it about the look in his eyes? The way they crawled over my body, pinning me in place? I would've sworn he knew everything about me, down to the color of my underwear. A chill ran through me when he moved closer, ignoring the crowd around us. "Run away if you think it will help, but I promise it won't."

How had he made that sound like a threat? How could he possibly be a threat to me? Somehow, I had regained control of my legs and wasted no time getting the hell away from him, almost knocking a toddler to the floor along the way. His revelation had unsettled something deep down, and to say I had been freaked out was an understatement.

If only he hadn't used her name. *Leila.* She was part of Dad's past before I ever came along. But she was very real, and they had once been married. I might have been able to dismiss the whole thing as a potential restraining order if it hadn't been for her name.

Was Miles trying to say he was my brother by Leila? Why would he come at me with such a nasty, almost threatening attitude? I had nothing to do with our parents' past.

If we had a half-brother, why wouldn't Dad tell us?

Did Mom know?

The question burned a hole in me as I sat there, toying with a glass of chardonnay and waiting for Valentina. I wouldn't normally have wine with lunch, but today, it felt necessary as my thoughts insisted on spiraling to a very dark place. If Mom didn't know there was another kid out there, I couldn't bring myself to hurt her by breaking the news. Was it my place to say anything? Should I talk to Dad first and figure out how much of what Miles said was true?

Why did it have to be a secret? I realized that was what bothered me the most. It felt like a dirty secret. If the whole thing was innocent, something that happened before Dad and Mom got together, why not come out and talk about it? Why hide Miles from us?

It made me think back on something I'd overheard Dad talking about a long time ago. I used to love hanging around when he was with his best friends, creeping up on his study while they were having guy talk or whatever it was. We weren't supposed to hang out nearby as they had a tendency to talk about things kids shouldn't hear.

Come to think of it, it was Mom and Dad's tenth wedding anniversary, and the big party they'd thrown at the apartment had wound down. Uncle Barrett and Dad had retreated to the study for brandy or something, and I had tiptoed behind them instead of going to my room to change out of my party dress. Uncle Barrett's voice had floated out through the half-open door. "Ten years. Did you ever see yourself reaching this point back when you were married to Leila?" He'd laughed.

"Don't speak that bitch's name," Dad had warned in a voice that made me wince, his anger evident.

"All I know is you became my fucking hero the night you turned her down in front of that whole party full of people." I had peeked in to see Uncle Barrett laughing, slapping a hand against Dad's back, and raising a glass like he was toasting him. "No wonder she ran to England when she knew you didn't want her back."

And Miles did have an English accent, didn't he? It still didn't mean anything. My father had not and would never cheat on Mom. That much I knew, and nobody could convince me otherwise. He was so in love with her, it was insane, and their relationship had taught me from a young age what to expect from a man. I would never settle for anything less than what they had.

So why keep Miles a secret? Why had I never heard his name until today? Was it possible that Leila tried to get Dad back and slept with him? Maybe she had deliberately gotten herself pregnant. Growing up the way we had surrounded by very wealthy people with complicated lives, it wouldn't have been the first time hearing a story like that.

The difference was the story had never involved my parents.

My life.

When Valentina showed up twenty minutes late, I knew something had to be up. My twin could be a real pain in the ass on a lot of things, but she was always punctual. "Sorry, sorry." She kissed my cheek before dropping into a chair and groaning like she'd just finished running a marathon. Even all worn out, she looked fantastic in a knee-length camel coat I didn't recognize.

"I'm borrowing that," I informed her, reaching out to test the weight and softness.

"I only bought it over the weekend," she informed me with another dramatic groan, growling before she yanked the fabric out of my hand. "Let me break it in first before you steal it."

"So what's up?" I asked, rolling my eyes when she took my glass of chardonnay and gulped the rest of it down.

Flipping her mahogany locks over one shoulder, she sighed like a woman with the weight of the world on her shoulders. Blue eyes similar to mine flashed as she explained, "You name it. I swear, everything that could go wrong today did. The new club I'm supposed to be promoting? The one opening in the meatpacking district?" My head bobbed. "They failed their final inspection, so the whole opening is getting pushed back weeks. Now I have to go and kiss ass with everybody who was supposed to be working with me on the run-up to the opening and be like sorry, my mistake, I'm working with a bunch of fucking amateurs."

I had no idea how she did her job. The girl kept so many plates spinning all at once and always managed to keep everything moving smoothly. "That sucks. I'm sorry."

"I'm going to need an entire bottle of this." She twisted in her chair, looking around for a server. When she caught the attention of someone, she held her glass up, then two fingers. Settling back down, she waved her hands, blowing out another sigh. "Sorry. How are you? Let's talk about something fun."

Well, there went my intended topic. "I texted Rose to let her know I'd need something for the gala," I told her instead of mentioning Miles.

Our mother's nonprofit was coming up on thirty years of empowering women, helping them find employment, and giving them the skills they needed to advance. It only seemed fitting to throw a huge celebration.

"Oh, hell, it's time for that already?" Shaking her head, she pulled out her phone to scroll through her calendar. "I swear to God, I'm losing it."

"It's weeks away," I reminded her. She was so organized when it came to her clients but not so much when it came to her own life. "But yeah, maybe you could ask Rose for a little help finding something to wear." Ari was fine for dressing Mom and her friends, but Rose understood what women our age liked.

"What about you?" When two glasses of wine arrived, she snatched one up without looking at it, her familiar blue eyes never leaving my face. That was the thing about being a twin. I couldn't hide anything from her any more than she could hide from me. I might be able to lie to other people, but not her. "You look as though you have something on your mind. All frowny and squinty."

Why waste time pretending? For one thing, she didn't need to hear about it right now. It might be better to keep this to myself and try to learn what I could about Miles. If this all turned out to be nothing, I didn't want to stir up shit that didn't need to be stirred.

"I'm fine. I really am," I insisted when she smirked like she didn't believe me. "It's just been a long day. I'm not feeling great."

"What, you mean staying with Mommy and Daddy isn't super refreshing?" She batted her eyelashes before snickering when I groaned. Mom had insisted I stay in my old room for a few weeks while my apartment was being renovated. Talk about being put on the spot. Refusal would've hurt her feelings. "You know, you don't have to stay there. Mom would get over it," she pointed out.

"That's not the problem." Dammit. I caught myself too late.

"What is the problem?" The gears were turning, for sure. It would've made things less cringeworthy if I'd come out and told her everything, but it would've meant dumping more stress on her already hectic day.

I could handle things on my own.

There was only one surefire excuse. "Cramps," I whispered, grimacing. When she sat back, nodding and frowning in empathy, it looked like I was home free, even if it was a complete lie.

"You'll feel better out on the slopes in a couple of weeks," she predicted.

Of course, I had almost forgotten about the trip to the family's cabin in Vermont. It had been Valentina's idea after we'd had so much fun hanging out with our cousins and friends at the Goldsmith estate in the Hamptons. It had meant all of us getting together for the first time since Colton and Rose started dating, and we'd had a blast. We hoped to get a little time in on the slopes prior to spring rolling around.

"You're right," I agreed with a genuine smile. "It'll be good to get up there for a while." And hopefully, by then, the whole Miles problem would be in my rearview mirror. I felt a little better by the time I started sipping my fresh wine, and my sister had me cracking up before long with stories from a recent disaster of a first date. It was enough that I could almost forget the whole thing.

That was until we parted ways so she could hurry off to a meeting. There was nothing stopping thoughts of Miles from rushing in and wrapping me in a fog of indecision. My heart was beating too fast as I stepped onto the sidewalk and took a deep breath of cool air. It didn't do much to clear my thoughts, and my pulse still pounded sickeningly. Was I having a panic attack? I'd never had one that I knew of, but I had heard them described, and this sure as hell felt like one —short of breath, sweating, the whole nine yards.

"You okay, sweetheart?" An older man noticed me practically clinging to a light pole, struggling to catch my breath. I nodded and gave him as much of a smile as I could. What was it people said about New Yorkers? We weren't nice, but we were kind. That man was another example. He continued on his way, and somehow, the distraction he had provided helped me regain control of myself. Not that I had forgotten my worries, but I could keep moving.

And once I started moving, there was one place I knew I had to be. If I had to wait a while for Dad to get home, so be it. I wanted to talk to him face-to-face and immediately.

Otherwise, there was no way I'd be able to function. As it was, I was hanging on by a thread.

After a short walk, I entered the apartment building I had called home for most of my life. The staff at the front desk had changed, but not much else had. There was something comforting about walking the familiar path to the elevator. The ability to move on autopilot, going through the motions I'd gone through so many times before, stabilized me.

Stepping off the elevator on the top floor, I opened the door to the sunshine-drenched penthouse. "Hello?" I called out, closing the door behind me, noting how quiet it was. I hadn't expected Mom to be around at this time of day—her work at the nonprofit normally kept her out until at least late afternoon or early evening, depending on her committments. Dad, however, had a more flexible schedule.

I was counting on him being home while Mom was out for the sake of privacy.

My heart sank a little when silence was the only response I received until his voice rang out. "In my study, Pumpkin." Normally, the sound of my childhood nickname would make me roll my eyes. Instead, I had to blink back the tears that came from out of nowhere. He couldn't have lied to us. I was twenty-eight years old and couldn't handle the idea of my father lying to me.

He met me in the doorway, smiling broadly as I approached. Aside from the silver threading through his dark hair and the lines at the corners of his eyes, he could have passed for a man twenty years younger.

It was that broad smile and the way he squeezed me when I gave him a hug that left me feeling heavy and conflicted again. He was in a fantastic mood, and I was here to potentially ruin it. "You're just the girl I wanted to see," he murmured, kissing the top of my head. "Well, you and your sister."

"What's going on?"

He was still smiling wide when he took my hand and tugged me into the room. "There's someone I want you to meet."

At first, I couldn't make sense of what I saw before me. It was like the man sitting in one of the leather chairs in front of Dad's oak desk, dressed in a dark suit this time, his dirty blond curls now tamed went out of his way to look nice for this meeting.

That didn't change anything. The knowing grin I'd seen earlier was firmly in place as Miles stood, straightening his suit jacket and extending a hand.

"Aria, I would like you to meet Miles Young." With his arm around my shoulder, Dad led me to where Miles waited for a handshake. "He's your stepbrother."

My stepbrother?

Mute with shock, I lifted my hand but barely felt the pressure as Miles engulfed it with his much larger hand. My stepbrother. It was true. Ice spread its way through my veins. Was I dreaming?

"Aria." Miles's rich voice practically dripped with what probably sounded genuine warmth to my father but sounded a lot like sarcasm to me when paired with the humor dancing in his gold-flecked eyes. "You have no idea how long I've waited for this."

2

MILES

Her open-mouthed, shocked expression was priceless. The only thing keeping me from laughing out loud was the memory of how long it had taken to get here, and that meant much more than the penthouse of the man whose name I'd heard for as long as I could remember.

"I'm sorry, Pumpkin." The man in question squeezed his daughter, whose icy hand I decided to release. "I know this comes as a shock."

Mom was right when she'd described him as a two-faced, arrogant asshole. How could he stand in front of me and pretend the surprise he'd pantomimed at my mother's grave was sincere? Did he truly believe she'd never explained—in detail—what went down between them?

Rather than wait for him to approach with his condolences, I went to him after the short graveside service drew to a close and cut to the chase. "I'm Miles Young. You must be my stepfather."

There was deep gratification in watching him react. The ticking of his jaw. The flared nostrils. He struggled to keep himself in check, for sure, but no man could be confronted by a past he tried to forget without reacting. "Your stepfather? How is that possible?" he asked, looking me over like he was searching for a resemblance to my mother.

So that was his choice. Pretending he never knew I existed. At that point, it was his word versus Mom's, and she could no longer tell her side of the story. No doubt he thought he was in the clear —the audacity of the greedy prick.

Raising my coat collar to shelter from an icy wind, I forced a chuckle for his sake. "You mean you had no idea I existed? I suppose it's understandable. From what I heard, I spent my earliest days in my grandmother's care while Mom worked."

"But she never..." His brow creased, dark eyes still darting over my face. "Why didn't I know about you?"

Still a liar after all these years. Some things never changed. "I couldn't tell you," I offered with a shrug. "The only person who could is no longer with us."

"How do you know who I am?" he asked. The slightest touch of suspicion leaked into the question, not that I was surprised. A naturally dishonest, cold-hearted prick would assume everyone operated as he did.

"There were five mourners at the grave," I reminded him. "Three of whom paid their respects as colleagues of mine. And you happen to look a lot like Magnus Miller, a man whose name I naturally googled once I learned he was my mother's husband back when I was a baby." Why he'd shown his face was a mystery. He'd abandoned her thirty years prior. Why care now? Maybe he wanted to confirm she was truly gone after seeing the obituary I'd sent to The New York Times.

Ex-wife of Manhattan Billionaire Dies in London.
Send donations in lieu of flowers.

I'd placed the ball in his court, and he'd decided to take a shot by flying out.

I hadn't expected him to play dumb, which meant a lot of ad-libbing on my part. He seemed to buy the explanation easily, some of the doubt draining from his penetrative stare. "You look a lot like her," he observed. "Let me take you to lunch. It seems we have a lot to catch up on."

That was all it took for my asshole stepfather to trust me— that and learning about the very profitable and still-growing Young Industries, of course. Once he knew I wasn't after his precious money, he let his guard down. "I still can't believe she'd keep you a secret," he murmured over a glass of scotch after hours spent catching up, as he put it.

He hadn't told me anything I didn't already know about him or his fucking family, though I did my best to feign interest and surprise when it applied.

Digging deep into my reserves of self-control, I suggested, "She may have been afraid of scaring you off. A single mother with a baby in diapers? How many young, wealthy men look to tie themselves down that way?"

"I would have liked to have a son." Staring into his glass, he murmured, "Knowing you were around might have changed a few things."

Naturally, he would say that. Anyone could make themselves a martyr with more than thirty years of silence. How convenient for him that Mom was no longer alive to throw his lies in his face. I would have to do it for her.

Aria stared at me, muscles twitching in her face while she attempted to process what had been dropped on her all at once. "My stepbrother." It was not a question but rather an attempt at clarity. She didn't want it to be true—that much was obvious when she had all but run from the coffee shop earlier. Perhaps I had overplayed my hand and frightened her too badly.

This was no empty-headed princess, no matter how spoiled and pampered she might have been. Still, when faced with the choice of approaching her or her twin, it seemed there was no contest. Valentina was sharper and more savvy. I'd observed her from afar and witnessed how she dispensed assholes at the clubs she promoted and events she planned. She would most likely have told me to get fucked if I approached her in public, charm or no charm.

The first encounter with Aria at the spin studio had sealed the deal. She'd noticed me, noticed the way I studied her, but didn't say a word. Same with the times she'd seen me throughout her normal routine. Her natural response had involved distrust and a touch of fear which kept her mouth shut. Instinct told me she would fit into my plan perfectly.

"I was as surprised as you are," I told her with a chuckle and a shrug. "There I was, thinking I was an only child all my life."

Magnus's affable grin told me my lies were believable. "Please, have a seat," he urged, gesturing toward the chair I'd left while directing his daughter toward the one beside it. He practically had to push down on her shoulders to make her sit, then ran a hand over her red-tinted locks. Obviously, a dye job. Nobody was born with burgundy hair.

"I don't understand." She looked up at her father with confusion and disbelief flashing across her face. A rather stunning face—delicate, symmetrical features, pouty lips, bright blue eyes that narrowed when they looked my way. "How do I have a stepbrother I never knew about?"

"It's a long story." Magnus wandered across the room

with its stuffed bookshelves and leather furniture. It was nearly as large as the first apartment Mom and I had shared. "You know I was married before I met your mother."

"Yeah. I remember you mentioning that." She couldn't help but glance my way, likely in memory of how we'd left things earlier.

Had she come here determined to get to the bottom of things and ask about my mom? It was clear I had gotten under her skin, no matter how she attempted to pretend otherwise.

Magnus turned with a glass of water in his hand and gave it to Aria, then patted her cheek and rounded the desk. He seemed like a very affectionate father. I wouldn't have guessed he had it in him.

A slight shift in her seat had me side-glancing in her direction. It was the girl with the glass of water who proved impossible to ignore. The glass trembled in her hands until she noticed me looking, then steadied as if by magic.

Sighing, Magnus took a seat. "Leila and I were divorced before I met your mother, Aria. She moved to England, cutting ties with everyone here. It wasn't until recently that I was aware of Miles's existence. For some reason, his mother chose to keep him a secret for the short time we were married."

I bit my tongue while his jaw tightened as if the memory angered him. As if he genuinely cared. "Now that I know," he concluded, "I hope we can get to know each other and, ideally, bring Miles into the family."

He had a way with words and glossing over several important points in the story. Like the fact that his dearest Evelyn clawed her way into their marriage, or even worse, that he knew about my existence when they were married but discarded me like last night's trash. It wouldn't do to reveal the way my stomach churned at his explanation. Somehow, I managed to maintain a neutral expression while observing Aria's reaction from the corner of my eye.

Immediately, her smooth brow furrowed as if she were troubled. Until then, she'd only looked like she'd swallowed something sour. "So he was born before your marriage. That would make him... thirty?"

"Nearly thirty-one," I murmured. She was doing the math, convincing herself there was no chance of us being related by blood. "From what I understand, I lived with my grandmother prior to the move overseas."

Magnus tipped his head to the side. I caught the resemblance between them when he frowned as she did. "Is there a problem with that?"

"No." Her troubled expression belied the statement. "I'm only wondering why we're hearing about him after all this time." Funny how she talked about me like I wasn't in the room. Typical wealthy brat.

"I'm getting to that. Unfortunately," Magnus continued, his voice going lower. "Miles's mother passed away several months ago."

Aria looked my way, her frown deepening. "I'm sorry for your loss," she murmured. The sort of thing people said to one another without thinking after that sort of announcement. She didn't mean it. If there was one thing life had forced upon me, it was a strong instinct when it came to people—seeing through their motivations and hearing what existed beneath their words. She was easy to read.

At that moment, she resented my existence from the crown of her head to the tips of her toes.

"When I flew out for the funeral, I met Miles." Magnus looked strangely proud when he turned my way as if he had anything to do with my life and education, or any of it. Men like him tended to take credit for what they played no part in—one of my mother's many lessons I had taken to heart. It had always been a better idea to heed her advice than ignore it. There weren't many things she'd detested worse than being ignored.

Aria groaned. "I thought you were out there to visit Uncle Charlie," she told him in a tone heavy with judgment. "You could have come out with the truth."

"It was my personal business," he said sharply, enough to make her shrink back a bit.

Finishing for him, I concluded, "And he generously invited me out to meet all of you. I doubt he intended for the visit to happen so soon, though. It happens I'd already planned the expansion of my company and had targeted New York as the natural starting point for breaching the states, so it seemed natural to stop in and say hello."

She couldn't have cared less. I wondered if she heard me at all over what raged in her head.

"I can't remember a more pleasant surprise. It's a shame your sister couldn't be here so I could introduce you both at the same time," Magnus pointed out to Aria.

It didn't seem she was listening. At the very least, she didn't react. It was obvious to me she was troubled. Magnus either didn't notice or pretended not to. I had no doubt of his skill at turning a blind eye to that which he didn't want to acknowledge. I was proof of that, wasn't I? We may not have been blood, but his influence had marked every aspect of my life.

All along, this man and his wife and daughters had lived in a palace. Every advantage and luxury had been theirs for the taking, while my mother and I had barely scratched out an existence.

"What is it you do, Aria?" I asked, feigning ignorance

while smiling like the sight of her didn't make me sick, as if this were the first time we'd set eyes on each other. Her silence on that point intrigued me. She believed in keeping things to herself and wasn't the sort of girl who ran to Daddy over every little thing. She struck me as being stoic—ironically, something I might have respected in anyone else. This pampered princess? It would be a cold day in hell when I respected her.

She struggled to find the words. "I... uh... I work at my mother's non-profit."

"Of course, that's right. I did a little research after meeting your father." Grinning at Magnus, I amended, "My *Stepfather.*"

The gamble paid off. She couldn't disguise the way she flinched at the use of the term. I hadn't expected this to be so much fun, digging at her. "A very impressive history, that non-profit," I continued. "What was the latest estimate of women and families who benefited from their involvement? It's well into the thousands by now, isn't it?"

"Tens of thousands," Magnus assured me with obvious pride. The prick had the nerve to puff out his chest as if he had anything to do with it. From what I'd learned, Evelyn was the brains in the relationship, taking her past trauma and turning it into something worthwhile. On the other hand, Magnus happened to luck out, thanks to his family's tech business. Not everyone had to work their way to the top like I did.

"Miles owns a highly successful tech company," Magnus explained. He was almost bragging by the sound of it. Why? He never gave a damn about me until the moment we'd locked eyes from opposite sides of my mother's grave. He'd feigned ignorance, pretending he'd never heard of me until then. It seemed he was maintaining the charade now. Did he think I'd never had a conversation with Mom about him?

"He met a rich man's sister and decided he could do better than a model with a kid." Her voice echoed in my head like a favorite song long since memorized. *"She was some ugly duckling with a limp. But she had money, and if there's one thing the rich love, it's other rich people. The greedy bastard left us with nothing. He humiliated me. I had no choice but to leave New York with you after that."*

Only the memory of everything she'd sacrificed for us was enough to keep me from vaulting over the desk and driving my fist into the smug bastard's face until it was unrecognizable, sitting here surrounded by luxury while his ex-wife lived in poverty for decades before I was able to provide for her. All because she was an up-and-coming model and not an heiress.

Like spoiled little Aria, who considered working at her mother's foundation a job and clearly bristled when I looked her way. "I'm looking forward to us getting to know each other better," I told her, fighting back a grin when her mouth tightened in obvious disagreement. Poor baby. Was this the only time she had ever come up against adversity?

She didn't trust me, and she was right not to. The girl had instincts almost as sharp as my own if she took a look at me and saw trouble. She had no idea how much trouble I could be.

Taking in her tight body took my thoughts down another, but no less dangerous, path. Had this uptight little brat ever been properly fucked? She deserved it with a body like that, with tits so perky they practically demanded to be worshiped. I'd admired her peach of an ass during our spin classes, watching her from behind. I imagined working her into a sweat, this time with me between her legs rather than a bike.

"If you want to know Aria better, you should hang around here a bit," Magnus offered, snapping me out of my untimely fantasy. "She's staying with us while her apartment is being renovated. I can't lie. It's nice to have her with us again."

"Dad..." She shook her head, giving him the smile a much-beloved child gives their parent when they feel exasperated.

I could barely keep a hold of myself. My brain was on fire, my body humming once the seed of an idea took root and began to grow, almost exploding in a series of branches that flowered all at once. Could I pull it off? There was only one way to find out. "Don't take that for granted," I urged her while almost trembling in anticipation. I had to be careful. "It must be nice having somewhere comforting to turn to when you're left without a home."

Would he bite the bait I dangled in front of him? So far, he had practically fallen over himself to be the generous, benevolent benefactor—the loving stepfather.

The man was entirely too easy to predict. "Where are you staying now that you've crossed the pond?" he asked, folding his hands on top of the desk while wearing a studious look as if he was in the middle of expanding his already voluminous investment portfolio.

Somehow I managed to refrain from rolling my eyes at his unimaginative turn of phrase. "Oh, I'm crashing at The Plaza at the moment. Still looking for something long-term."

Come on, come on, ask me. I could feel it in the air like an electrical charge before a lightning strike.

"Nonsense!" he boomed, shaking his head. "There's

more than enough room here. Why don't you stay with us until you find a permanent place for yourself?"

Got him.

"Dad," Aria muttered. When she caught me looking, she did a poor job of rearranging her expression into something that didn't look quite as murderous. "I'm sure Miles can stay literally anywhere he wants to stay. I mean, if he's half as successful as you're making him out to be. Don't insult him."

I made a point of glancing her way before I spoke, intent on giving him the impression I was refusing with her shitty attitude in mind. "Really, you're too generous," I insisted. "You have already been so kind. I couldn't impose."

"It's not an imposition if I'm asking point-blank for you to stay." I opened my mouth, prepared to offer another half-hearted and completely empty protest, but he was hearing none of it. "My mind is made up. I expect you to get your things together back at The Plaza. I'll have someone over there to transport everything as soon as you're ready."

"Well..." I glanced at Aria again, underlining my concern over her feelings before shrugging. "To tell you the truth, I would like the opportunity to get to know all of you better. Mom was the only family I had, so finding all of you has been a gift."

"I'm sure the same goes for us." I caught the way his gaze landed and lingered on his daughter, who had now settled for glaring murderously at her father with him either pretending not to notice or, more likely, being completely oblivious. And he was supposed to be some sharp-witted billionaire? He couldn't even see what was taking place in front of him.

If anything, it was my duty to set him straight. I would open his eyes and force him to see how his thoughtless, selfish choices had rippled out through the decades and were now coming home to roost.

"It shouldn't take me very long," I offered as I stood, followed by Magnus. "I only brought enough for two weeks or so, intending to send for the rest once I found a permanent home."

"Take all the time you need." He rounded the desk before placing a hand on my shoulder. No doubt it was supposed to be a comforting, friendly gesture. What a shame it turned my stomach.

"Dad, can I talk to you for a minute?" Aria had missed the memo regarding how to behave politely, choosing instead to scowl at me, tugging her father's sleeve.

It was unfortunate his phone rang when it did. He scowled, turning back to the desk. "I have to take this. I've been waiting for this call all day. Don't worry," he told her, giving her an absent pat on the cheek. "I'll find you later, and we can talk. If you'll excuse me."

I knew what that meant, and so did she. With a soft grunt, she turned and marched from the room, the heels of her ankle boots striking the hardwood hard enough that I snickered to myself. Spoiled little bitch. She didn't know what to do with herself now that Daddy hadn't stopped the world at her request.

We were no more than a half-dozen strides into the hall when she whirled on me. The composed mask she had been wearing in her father's office fell away. This was the real Aria, all flashing eyes and flushed cheeks, her perfect teeth bared in a snarl before she jabbed a finger against my chest. Goddamn, she was hot, so hot I looked forward to working her up this way for weeks to come.

"Listen..." she snarled, "... you might have him fooled, but not me."

"Excuse me?" I asked, all innocent, as I looked down at her finger. It would have been too easy to yank her close and make her think twice about poking the lion unless she knew she could handle the roar. "What is this all about?"

"Drop the act," she warned. "All your life, you didn't know him or any of us, and now you want to be part of the family? I'm sure you didn't mind finding out your mother's ex-husband is a billionaire. I'm sure that had *nothing* to do with it."

A billionaire who left his ex with nothing. Who abandoned her when something more interesting came along and conveniently ignored the fact of a child being involved. "Not everyone is as mercenary as you clearly are, Aria," I murmured, pride swelling in my chest when her face went pink, and she fell back a step. "As for money, I have all I'll ever need."

"Sure, keep playing innocent. It seems to be working so fucking well." She cast a doleful eye toward her father's closed door. "You are not going to take advantage of his kindness. I won't let you."

"Really, Aria, you're going to have to explain what you mean. I don't have the first idea."

Her cheeks went from pink to deep red. "You know damn well what I mean." Touching a hand to her chest, she whimpered out, "Oh, poor me, a rich tech guy with nowhere to stay. I don't have a family. *Let me invade yours.*"

"Is that what you're worried about? Are you afraid Daddy doesn't have enough time for you now that he's found the son he always wanted?" That might have been a mistake, but it came tumbling out before I could help it. It was unusual for me to take such a risk, but then her imperious attitude left me craving the satisfaction of watching her wither under my perceptive gaze. "Maybe you *should* be worried. He might want a son with business sense to manage his investments while you go to spin class and have your hair done. He may even add me to his will. That would put a crimp in your plans, I'd bet."

Her head snapped back like she'd been struck. "Fuck you," she whispered, trembling. "That is a foul thing to say. You're a foul person."

"I've been called worse things by people I've respected and who had a legitimate reason to sling slurs around." I sighed, tired of where this conversation was going. "Your name-calling doesn't matter to me, especially when I've done nothing to deserve it."

"I am not going to let you do whatever it is you have in mind," she warned, trailing me through the sprawling penthouse, her footsteps ringing out like gunshots.

The artwork on the walls would have put me through university twice over with thousands to spare, but they probably took it for granted.

"Is this the way to the door?" I asked over my shoulder, ignoring her.

"Yes," she growled out. "And if you know what's good for you, you'll walk through it and not come back."

"But Aria, I've been invited, remember?" It was almost impossible not to openly laugh at the impotent fury that twisted her features when I stopped at the door and turned to face her. "Look at it this way. We'll get to know each other better. Your father seems very keen on all of us being a family."

"You will never be part of my family," she warned.

"Is that a threat? I can't quite tell." Chuckling, I opened the door and headed for the elevator. "We can work it all out when I come back. And *I will*," I assured her.

"It's your funeral." She slammed the door between us,

and it was a relief to let out the laugh I'd been holding back, even as my dick twitched at the challenge she presented. I would surely remember her heaving tits later, alone, jerking off to the memory of sizzling heat that seemed to spring to life out of nowhere when we were face-to-face.

It wouldn't be a hardship to take advantage of our chemistry and the fact she was so very easy on the eyes.

Magnus had no idea who he'd welcomed into his home. The man who would tear his perfect family to pieces.

I could hardly wait to get started.

3

ARIA

"So that's it. Our brand-new stepbrother took one of the guestrooms on the first floor like he actually belonged here." His suite was directly beneath mine. With that in mind, I stomped my feet, pacing at the foot of my bed. Immature? Of course. Funny how certain situations could make a person not give a shit about what was mature and what wasn't.

"I think it's cool." Valentina's laughter filtered through the phone's speaker when I grunted at her ridiculous assertion. "We have a stepbrother now. We should be happy Dad seems so happy."

The worst part was she had a point. I knew better. "Only because Dad can't see the real Miles."

"Oh? And you can? You have this huge amount of insight into him that Dad doesn't?" The way she scoffed didn't make things any better.

Gritting my teeth and stomping harder, I replied, "It's hard to explain."

"Since when have you had a hard time explaining something to me?"

That was the thing. I couldn't remember ever feeling this disconnected from my twin. We practically shared a brain, or we had before some two-faced tech bro decided to get on a plane and insert himself into our lives. "This is complicated. I told you how he found me at the spin studio. Why couldn't he have told me who he was? Why did he have to be so weird and creepy about it for weeks? He was starting to scare me."

"Maybe because he was afraid you would react the way you're reacting right now," she suggested. "He probably wanted to wait until Dad was around so you wouldn't rip off his head."

"Yeah, I might still do that anyway."

"I think you're overreacting," she said with a sigh.

"And I think you're gaslighting me a little bit," I retorted, spinning on my heel to walk back across my old bedroom. Ironic that I felt like a teenager again in this room, only this time, I wasn't pissed off because Penelope Schwartz copied my idea for a topic on our final English paper. This was real, grown-up shit with actual consequences. "I told you that crack he made about the will and how Dad now has the son he wanted. That doesn't strike you as being wrong?"

"I mean, yeah, it was in poor taste," she agreed. "But you were acting all belligerent and whatnot."

"How would you know? You weren't there."

"I can see you in my head. Your chin jutting out and everything." She laughed while I checked my reflection in the mirror over the dresser as I passed. Sure enough, my chin was sticking out. "He was trying to get to you. That's all."

How easy would it have been to accept her explanation and move on? My pacing slowed as I realized I wanted to. It would've been simple to accept his arrival and intentions at face value.

The only problem was I had seen him before that meeting in Dad's study. I had felt his... resentment? It was the closest thing to what had shone in his burning glare more than once at spin class and on the sidewalk. I'd seen it again in the hall outside the study. There was no explaining the sort of thing a person had to feel to understand.

"Miles Young?" she asked, and I grunted confirmation, waiting only a few moments before I heard Valentina's sound of approval coming through the phone. "Well, I'll say one thing. He's fucking hot."

It looked like we had both reverted to being teenagers. Groaning, I asked, "Because that matters?"

"Uh... yeah. It does. I have eyes. I'm allowed to appreciate what I see." She mumbled something as though she was reading from an article. "Oh, he's the guy who designed that new algorithm thingy. I remember hearing about that. And he's big into AI."

"Yeah, he would come up with new ways for humanity to be squeezed out, wouldn't he? I'm telling you," I insisted when she laughed. "There is something really wrong with the guy."

"Listen. I hear what you're saying, I really do. But Dad isn't some senile old man," she reminded me. "He doesn't need you to protect him."

"If you had seen the way he was smiling at Miles like he was proud of him, you would think differently." The memory made me shudder in revulsion, the way I would if I had touched a snake. Funny, how bringing him to mind was that of a snake.

"Yeah, okay. I can see that being a little uncomfortable."

"Thank you," I mumbled.

I should've known she wouldn't leave it there. "But think of it this way. After everything we pieced together about that Leila woman over the years, doesn't it seem like he might not have had the best upbringing? Maybe that's where Dad is coming from," she concluded. "He feels sorry for Miles because he knows who his mother was. We don't know what Miles might have gone through."

It was unusual for her to be so willing to extend grace. Usually, she would have been at my side, demanding an explanation. Like why we'd never heard of Miles and what he thought he'd get out of worming his way into our family.

It didn't take long for me to understand my mistake. "Mom already got to you, didn't she? You already knew what happened before we got on the phone." I groaned, slapping a palm to my forehead. It had taken hours to get a hold of my sister, and I had practically gone crazy waiting to fill her in.

"Why are you treating this like it's warfare or something? Mom spoke to me," she amended. "She gave me the bullet points. That's where Dad is coming from. He feels sorry for Miles and wishes he could have been an influence in his life."

"Why? He doesn't owe Miles a damn thing."

"How the hell would I know?" she snapped. "Man, you are determined to look for the worst possible explanation for all of this. There's a good chance he doesn't have any kind of ulterior motive at all."

It was obvious I was talking to a wall. "Fine. Whatever you say," I replied.

The sound of her groan was as familiar as my reflection. "Don't be that way."

Settling down on the foot of the bed, I asked, "What? I'm being unreasonable, so I'm going to let it go now."

"If I thought you were actually letting it go, it would be one thing."

"It'll be fine," I flatly insisted. "The end."

"And then you shut down on me," she said with a sigh. "Just give the guy a chance. I'd better go. I have a few more emails to send out before I collapse." There was still tension on my side when we ended the call, wishing each other a good night.

In the entire world, there was nothing I hated more than being underestimated or overlooked. I had always been the quieter twin. I kept things to myself. And this was why. Sometimes, it wasn't worth putting myself out there and speaking my mind.

I hadn't been hungry at dinner—my stomach was in no shape to handle food. Now, though, I could've used a snack. From what I understood, Miles had come back from the hotel and was probably in the middle of getting settled. There was no reason we had to run into each other with his suite being far from the kitchen, at the other end of the first floor from the living room, dining room, and kitchen. I didn't have to venture any deeper into the penthouse while he was around. He could have that entire half of the floor to himself, including Dad's study. They could sit around and drink scotch and pat each other on the back or whatever it was men did behind closed doors.

I pulled a silk robe over my pajamas, twisting my hair into a bun on top of my head while padding barefoot down the stairs that opened onto the foyer. The memory of Miles laughing at me in that very spot was still clear and sharp. I turned my gaze away from the door, growling. Where did he get off being so smug and acting like he knew me?

The living room was dark, and only a few sconces lit the

hall leading deeper into the penthouse. I could have done this blindfolded. Not much had made me smile that day, at least not since I'd found Miles sitting in Dad's study, pretending he owned the place. I could smile at the memory of me and Valentina sneaking downstairs for a snack when we were kids, tiptoeing down the hall, trying like hell not to make noise.

The sound of the water suddenly turning on up ahead in the kitchen made me stumble a little. Shit. Was he in there? My heartbeat slowed when Mom's soft humming followed, and knowing she was still up gave me a sense of peace the conversation with my sister definitely had not.

"Hey, you." She smiled from where she stood in front of the stove, turning on the heat beneath the kettle. I had seen her there so many times over the years. The fact that she looked as young as she always had left me feeling ten years old again. If only. "Do you want some tea?"

"No, thanks. I figured I would grab a little something to eat." Kissing her cheek on the way to the refrigerator reminded me how glad I was to have a little time back home. Even if it meant having to see Miles and constantly being reminded of how much he had creeped me out when he first came to town.

"Oh, good. You had me worried there when you said you didn't want dinner." Then she laughed softly and shook her head. "Here I am, treating you like a little girl again. It's not easy to remember you're all grown up."

I didn't feel so grown up. When was the last time I was this worried and uneasy? "I know you were talking to Valentina earlier." I opened one of the cabinets, my eye on her. Her shoulders sank, then shook with soft laughter. She knew I had figured her out.

"Somebody had to tell her what happened today," she

pointed out. "I happened to get a hold of her before you did."

"Was it true what you said about Dad?"

"It depends on what you think I said." The woman had mastered the art of the no-answer answer. While it cracked me up when she pulled that shit with Dad, I wasn't so amused now.

"That he felt bad for Miles?" I asked.

"It's true. A lot of things happened back then before you were born. It was a lifetime ago," she murmured while staring off over my shoulder, seeing the past. "Leila was no picnic. And considering Miles has no other family, it seems only right to your father to bring him into the fold."

"I'm not trying to be selfish." Hauling myself onto the counter, I unwrapped a protein bar and took a bite while Mom fixed her herbal tea.

"I know you're not, sweetie. And I know you must have been shocked when you suddenly found out you have a stepbrother."

He's not my stepbrother. I didn't want to come out and say it, knowing I'd only look worse if I did. "Are you sure you're okay with it?"

"As far as I'm concerned, the more the merrier. One day, you'll be an empty nester," she predicted with a touch of sadness in her voice. "And it will make you very happy to have a new life under the roof. Trust me."

Did it have to be this life? There was no way of getting my point across unless I flat-out told Mom how we had already started off on the wrong foot. How he'd sort of scared me a little. She would only wave it off, clicking her tongue, basically patronizing me.

"Give him a chance." She picked up her mug and gave

me a one-armed hug on her way out to the hall. "There's always more than meets the eye. Don't forget that."

That wasn't the problem. I knew there was more than met the eye with Miles. It was everybody else who needed to get their goddamn vision checked. What would it take for them to see? Did something awful have to happen? I didn't want to think about it.

So, of course, it was all I could think about as I left the kitchen and turned down the hall. Not ten steps into my journey, a deep voice filled the air behind me. "Well, well. Look at you. Nice pajamas."

Fucking hell. I'd have to ignore my hunger next time. Turning, I looked him up and down. "Nice jacket," I countered. Nice everything, really. As furious and distrusting as I was, I could admit he looked good in a black leather jacket, jeans, and heavy boots. His hair had that tousled quality again, and it paired nicely with his smirk.

"Thanks. I'm on my way out for a ride. Do you like motorcycles?" he asked with laughter in his voice.

"I've never cared either way." It wasn't a lie. I wasn't into cars either.

"Have you ever been on one?"

I rolled my eyes and muttered, "It's not on my bucket list." Wasn't he on his way out? Why take the time to irk me?

"Perhaps I can change your mind on the experience." He folded his arms, his smirk turning into a full grin. It was funny the way heat erupted in my core at the sight of it, though the way he deepened his voice didn't hurt either. "You don't know if you enjoy something until you try it. And then you might find yourself addicted. I've been known to have that effect." I would've sworn his eyes went a deeper shade of green before narrowing with deeper meaning.

He's hitting on me now? Following the rollercoaster of a

day I'd had, there wasn't much more of him I could take. "Careful," I warned, meeting his gaze without flinching. "You shouldn't talk that way to your *stepsister*."

"That's right." With a brief nod, he said, "That is who you are. It's nice to hear you say it. Maybe you and I can get along after all."

"Do me a favor and hold your breath until the time comes," I replied. His soft laughter was as good as nails dragging down a chalkboard as he passed me, sauntering toward the front door like he owned the place. It was better to let him leave without trying to get in the last word since I was already risking my teeth by grinding them as hard as I did.

∼

"That's really amazing! You have a brother! You always said you wanted one."

I was starting to believe everybody in my life was going through mass delusion. It was one thing for my immediate family to be completely blind, but I had expected better from Sienna. She was a public relations expert, for God's sake. She had to know how two-faced and unreliable people could be. She had seen the worst of her clients for years. Yet there she was, all wide-eyed and eager to hear more about this supposed addition to my family.

"He's only my stepbrother," I reminded her with a groan. "Even then, does it count? Dad didn't even know about him while they were married. We're talking about a major technicality."

"Obviously, that doesn't matter to your dad. I think it's nice he wants to bring Miles in and make him a part of things. Your dad isn't an idiot," she pointed out. We had different opinions on that one. "He knows what he's doing."

"I'm not so sure. People do crazy things when they feel guilty."

"Anyway, at least we know now why Miles was being all weird toward you before." She looked at the clock on the wall, which stated we had another few minutes until class started. "Where is he, I wonder? I would like to meet him."

Maybe he wouldn't show up. It was bad enough I had to see him at home. It would've been nice to have an excuse for a reprieve.

It looked like my luck was shit all the way around. He hurried in with a minute to spare, smiling wide when he spotted me chatting with Sienna. He looked like a shark who'd spotted his next meal, or was I telling myself that because I didn't want to believe he had good intentions? Dammit, I was letting everybody get in my head. I had to follow my gut on this.

Sienna had no such problems. "So you're Miles?" She extended a hand as soon as he was close enough. "Aria told me all about you. To think, you were taking class with us, and you had this secret."

The snarky, arrogant prick who had taunted me last night was replaced by the charming, affable guy I'd met in Dad's study. It was like he had two personalities. "I didn't want to come on too strong, too fast," he explained as he shook her hand. "And you are?"

"Oh, sorry! I was too busy admiring that accent of yours." She giggled before replying, "Sienna Black. Aria's cousin."

His brows shot up. "So we're cousins! The family expands." The prick even had the nerve to smile at me like he was daring me to be anything but positive. Considering rage was burning a hole in me, it was better to keep my mouth shut.

"Something like that," she agreed with a laugh. "I'm sure we'll get along fine, so long as you don't think you can outpace me." She patted the bike and narrowed her eyes in a challenge.

"I would never think of telling a woman I could beat her at anything," he promised before they shared a laugh that made my skin crawl. Seriously? He was charming her too. It was almost enough to make me wonder if I was making all of this up in my head.

No. He'd given me a bad feeling from day one, way before I knew who he was. I wasn't about to forget his nasty comments about Dad wanting a son to manage his money either. Nobody said something like that unless they were already thinking along those lines, plotting to take what wasn't rightfully theirs.

I was not about to believe he had anything but bad intentions. All I had to do was find out what they were and how to stop him.

4

MILES

Finally, I could get out of that fucking penthouse and stop feeling so suffocated.

Until now, I wouldn't have imagined it possible to feel trapped while inside a palace like the one I'd stayed at the past several days. Work had kept me busy enough that I could get away with escaping when I needed to. It wasn't that I was uncomfortable—far from it.

It was the way the comfort sickened me. Aria had grown up there. Probably running up and down the hall with her sister or watching movies in the obnoxious home theater Magnus had urged me to use on the second floor because not only did the family need a two-story penthouse, they couldn't be bothered to see a film with ordinary people in a theater—pampered little rich girls while I had gone hungry so many nights, crying myself to sleep, wondering when Mom would come home. Hoping she would bring something to eat. Hoping like fuck, I wouldn't fall asleep again with a growling stomach and the taste of salty tears.

Who could blame me for needing an evening to myself?

It wasn't like I was missing much at the penthouse anyway. Aria was out for the night. I'd heard her loudly announce her plans to her mother when she'd caught sight of me coming in from my new office down in The Battery. If the girl wanted me to believe she didn't care about my presence, she was doing a piss-poor job of it. But that was all right. She added a bit of excitement to my vocation of making sure Magnus regretted ever breaking my mother's heart.

"He didn't want us." Lingering at a traffic light, the bike rumbling beneath me, I could hear her plaintive cries as clearly as if she were in my ear. *"I couldn't have you around because he didn't want to be a father. Of course, as soon as he locked down that limping little nothing, he decided he wanted to be one after all. How convenient for him."*

The instant the light went green, I shot forward, leaving the cars around me in my dust. She had never come out and said it, but I'd understood subtext even at an early age. I had cost Mom her husband. If it hadn't been for me, they might have made it work and started a family of their own, the way Magnus had with Evelyn.

The memory wasn't what left me feeling as bitter as I did that evening, tearing through the bustling city, snippets and flashes of life passing around me. All those years, I'd heard nothing but terrible things about Evelyn Black. She was a homewrecker, a whore, an ugly duckling who'd known she had nothing to offer but her brother's wealth. *"Magnus always did have a weak spot for broken things."* Mom had laughed many times. *"She was counting on that when she seduced him."*

Except Evelyn didn't strike me as the woman my mother had described. Then again, roughly thirty years had passed since she sank her claws into Magnus. Time had a way of changing people, so it wasn't an impossibility.

"We're having a family dinner with Aria and Valentina next week." Evelyn had made it a point to tell me when we crossed paths earlier. Aria had all but snarled, then shot her mother a sharp look which she ignored. "We would love it if you could join us. Nothing outrageous, just a nice dinner here at home. I know Magnus would be happy to have you join us."

Aria certainly wouldn't be, which was another reason why I'd gladly accepted. There was nothing as satisfying as watching someone walk headfirst into their own demise. It would be like the rabbit welcoming the hunter's snare. And they didn't have the faintest idea.

Why would they? They had never given a moment's thought to anyone but themselves. That, if for no other reason, was more than enough cause to set them straight on a great many things. They needed to have their eyes opened.

I wasn't in the mood for polite company tonight. I'd had more than enough of that.

That is what led me to what I could only describe as a seedy part of town, and that was being generous. I doubted pampered little Aria ever set eyes on anything like this. Apartment buildings where half the windows were boarded up, litter clogging the gutters. Rats scurrying across the street and down the sidewalks. Approaching a corner, I spotted two women attempting to strike up conversations with drivers in cars paused at a stop sign. No doubt one of Magnus's precious daughters would look at women like that and recoil.

I couldn't help but think of Mom as I continued on, the two of them whistling in appreciation as I passed. She had never been that desperate. She'd always sworn there were levels to which she would not sink, even for my sake. I was glad of that even now. I didn't know if I could carry that level of guilt around for the rest of my life.

Up ahead was a bar, and I wondered as I approached how many years its faded sign had served as a beacon for the thirsty, lonely, and dependent. This was where I wanted to be. Around real people, where I could stop pretending for a little while.

It didn't matter how much money I made, and I had made quite a lot of it. So much so that I hadn't blinked an eye when I purchased my fully customized Harley-Davidson CVO Road Glide Limited. And I didn't mind leaving it parked outside a dive bar in the middle of The Bronx either. I could always buy another. That was one thing I had sworn to myself as a kid during those long, hungry nights when I never knew when Mom would be home from one of her many jobs.

When I'm rich, I'm going to buy whatever I want and do whatever I want, and I'll have so much money it won't matter.

That goal was now a reality. Fine-tuning my algorithm had been my ticket to millions in profit in the last year alone. Now that I was taking the firm internationally with AI advancements, there was no reason to believe I wouldn't add another couple of zeros to those figures before long. At least, that was my intention.

Yet as I strolled through a rusty door that squealed hideously on its hinges, I was a regular man. A thirsty man in search of a distraction.

Fuck, I loved it. The stench of stale beer in the air. The slight stickiness of the floors—more than once, it took conscious effort to pull the soles of my boots away from the splattered boards. By all rights, I should have recoiled in horror at the stained tiles overhead, yellowed and somehow still stinking of smoke years after smoking had been banned in public establishments. It was dark, dingy, and at least three of the men sitting at the scarred bar looked like they would enjoy the chance to kick my ass.

I would've enjoyed the chance to see how far they felt they could go. It would not have been the first time some piece of trash had taken a look at me and assumed I would make an easy target. I had been fighting for my life early on, and it had never stopped. Only the opponents had.

"Stella Artois with a Jack back," I told the bartender, ignoring the way his brow creased at the sound of my accent. That was usually the way of it whenever I visited this level of establishment.

The music blasting from the old-fashioned jukebox in the far corner was loud and grating, but it was the raucous laughter of the women drunkenly dancing that drew my attention—four of them, clearly friends, utterly involved in their good time.

One in particular intrigued me—a tall, leggy brunette in a skirt short enough to make the hem flirt with the curve of her ass cheek. Her heavy makeup concealed what might have been a pretty face without it.

One of the women she was with must have noticed the attention I was giving them since before long, the brunette glanced my way after her friend whispered in her ear. We understood each other from the moment our eyes met, and a silent communication passed between us. I wasn't looking for more than a good time, and neither was she.

Glossy lips curved in an inviting smile before she began crossing the room in a pair of sky-high heels. She wore a tight top with dozens of cutouts exposing vast expanses of olive skin, the fabric thin enough that her nipples were plainly visible. If they got much harder, they would tear through. For all I knew, that could've been the point. Everything about her was designed to attract attention, and she had certainly attracted mine.

Of all times for Aria's curves and sassy mouth to invade my senses, threatening to take over my thoughts, this wasn't it.

She wouldn't be caught dead in such an outfit, though I had no doubt she would've looked like a wet dream come to life. It had to be the way she closed herself off that made her so painfully attractive and me so painfully hard half the time. I was no better than a young man going through puberty when it came to her. The challenge she presented made her that much more tantalizing.

At the moment, all she did was make the woman in front of me look like a sad, worn-out hag. I didn't want that. Tonight was all about working out the tension that had built in me over days spent among so-called civilized people.

"Hey, handsome," she purred upon reaching me, propping her elbows on the bar top and pushing her tits up and out like an offering. "Never seen you around here before. What are you doing slumming?"

Another thing I appreciated about women like her was their candor. It was refreshing after wasting so much precious time around women who couldn't be bothered to be upfront. "If I'm slumming, then you're slumming," I pointed out, winking. "You shouldn't sell yourself short."

Her mouth fell open a bit. I had seen this reaction before. "Oh, that accent is the sexiest thing I've ever heard," she breathed out. "Say something else."

Why hadn't Aria reacted that way when we met? Fuck, I was allowing the girl to cockblock me when she was nowhere near this seedy dive. "What do you wanna hear?"

"Anything." She swayed nearer, bringing the scent of beer and cheap perfume with her. "Just so long as you're talking."

"I would like to buy you a drink, but I am not in the habit of buying drinks for people whose names I don't know." I cocked my head to the side, smiling at how flustered she'd become. "What do you think? Can we do something about that, love?" I was playing it up. There was no resisting the impulse.

"Fuck, that is hot. I'm Jamie." Her red nails danced up my arm, then back down again. "How about you, gorgeous? What's your name?"

"Willam." Because I would be fucked if I gave this girl more information about myself than was strictly necessary. All it would take was hearing my name in business news for her to decide we had a relationship. Then again, what was I thinking? Something told me Jamie didn't spend much free time perusing the latest developments in the business world. The latest reality TV scandal was probably much more her speed.

"It's nice to meet you, Willam." The way the name rolled off her tongue sounded like sex or at least the promise of it. I had watched countless women twist themselves into knots, trying to attract the attention of men they believed were weak or stupid enough to fall for their bullshit. The only thing they had going for them was the possibility of trapping a wealthy man and squeezing every last dime out of him before moving on to the next target.

"Likewise," I told her, smiling to myself when she released a soft groan of hunger and desire. I could have taken her then and there on top of that filthy bartop, and she wouldn't have protested.

"Do you like motorcycles?" I asked, chuckling when her

eyes widened. "Mine is parked outside. It's a limited-edition Harley-Davidson, fresh off the factory floor. Are you familiar with the brand?"

"Who isn't?" Something told me I could have made up a name, and she would have salivated. Again, Aria came to mind, this time the memory of her neutral reaction to what normally made women cream their panties. Why was everything involving her so damned difficult? I needed to get her out of my head, or she would ruin my night.

"I would love to take you for a ride." My attention landed on her mouth and those glossy lips. She would leave a red ring around my cock before the night was over, and that part of my anatomy twitched in anticipation.

"Baby, you can take me anywhere," she purred, sliding her hand up my arm and over my shoulder, then draping her arm around my neck. "Anywhere you want. And you can put it anywhere you want," she added in a breathy voice, her lids lowering.

The idea of flying through the night with this woman wrapped around me was almost fully formed in my mind's eye when a buzzing from my jacket pocket tore my attention from her. "Excuse me." She leaned away while I located the device and checked the ID. *Unknown number*. "Hold that thought," I told the woman whose name I had already forgotten while draining what was left in my glass.

It was much too loud inside. I answered the call on my way through that screeching door, stepping out into the cool night air before greeting the caller. "Miles Young."

"Miles? This is Colton Black. I think you met my sister a few days ago."

Of course, Evelyn's nephew. "Cousin Colton," I replied, injecting much more warmth into my voice than was present. "It's good to hear from you." He had probably gotten my number from Magnus.

"Are you busy tonight?" he asked. There were voices in the background, many overlapping, like he was calling from a club or a bar. Something told me it was far different from the one in front of which I stood.

Glancing toward the door I had walked through, remembering the woman inside, I replied, "Not very."

"How about coming out and having drinks with us? Everybody wants to meet you."

Interesting. "Who is everybody?"

"Our whole group. My sister is here with another one of our cousins and a couple of friends. And, of course, your stepsisters," he added, chuckling like it was a joke.

Aria was with him. This night had become much more interesting, and my thickening dick certainly agreed. "I would like to meet everyone," I told him, grinning to myself at the idea of how pissed off she would be when I showed up wherever they were.

She never bothered hiding her contempt. I would see if she could hide it in front of her friends and family without her parents' presence.

Naturally, I would make her look like the little fool she was. By the end of the night, the rest of them would sing my praises and assure her I would never do anything to the family I was so glad to be part of.

"I'll send you the location," Colton assured me.

"I'll be looking for it." By the time I ended the call, I was brimming over with anticipation. This would be a hell of a lot more fun than fucking some nameless skank in the hopes of working a little frustration out of my system.

I was about to set off for my bike when another idea

occurred to me. Would it work? It might take a little convincing, but I had no doubt I could sell it.

It was time to up the stakes a bit, and Colton Black may have inadvertently given me exactly what I needed to do just that.

Pulling my phone free from my pocket again, I placed a call, grinning in anticipation of what was to come.

5

ARIA

"Are you fucking joking?" It wasn't that I wanted to rip my cousin Colton's head off. I wouldn't have minded the opportunity to kick it around a little bit if someone else did, though. He had the nerve to look surprised at my reaction as if there was nothing out of the ordinary about inviting the asshole out with us.

"Honestly, in Colton's defense, I don't see what the problem is." Rose slid an arm around Colton's waist, touching the side of her head to his arm. No big surprise, the fact that she would take his side after he came in and announced he'd invited Miles to have drinks with us. He could break a beer bottle and slice someone open with the jagged end, and she would probably insist he had a good reason for it. Love did that to people. It made them willing to turn a blind eye to the obvious.

"Aria doesn't like him, and that's all we need to know." At least my sister was willing to speak up for me, leaning over to pat my knee before reaching for the wine glass on the round table in the center of our circle of chairs.

This was one of our usual spots, somewhere low-key

enough that we could kick back and have a good time without our chairs vibrating, thanks to the deafening music. No drunk bodies falling against us either.

"What do you think of him?" Evan winked at me, then turned his attention back to my sister. I scowled, and he pretended he couldn't see me out of the corner of his eye. The way his lips twitched told another story.

Valentina shrugged, sipping her wine. "I don't know. I guess he's all right. She's the one who has to spend time with him at home."

"It's not like we're hanging out," I made sure to tell everybody in case they figured we were having heart-to-heart conversations over our morning coffee.

"Maybe if you did hang out with him a little bit, you would get to know him, and it wouldn't seem like such a big deal to have him around." Sienna shrugged when I shot her a look. "What? He seemed okay when I met him."

It took everything I had to sound neutral. "We just didn't get off on the right foot, that's all." The longer this conversation dragged on, the more uncomfortable it made me. I needed to end it before Miles showed up at Colton's invitation.

Valentina must have noticed my discomfort because she jumped in before anybody could answer. "So, let's talk Vermont. Who's bringing what? How is everybody getting up there?"

My relief was short-lived. It was my cousin, Lucian, who noticed him first, lifting his head and nudging Colton. "This him?" he asked, jerking his chin toward something over my shoulder. Yes, it was Miles. How did I know without looking?

I felt the prick.

Noah stood, extending a hand. "Noah Goldsmith," he

announced, wearing a warm smile. "So you're the guy behind Young Industries."

Miles's empty laughter made my skin crawl. "That would be me. And you're the guy behind Goldsmith Real Estate."

"Don't hog him." Sienna nudged her boyfriend aside to offer Miles a brief side hug.

A fucking hug.

I was hallucinating, right? He was still standing close to my chair, meaning I had a front-row seat to what sounded so obviously fake to my ears.

Was I the one with the problem?

Glancing around, I saw nothing but general friendliness from everybody. They introduced themselves, explained who they were, and asked him questions about himself. Was this his first trip to New York? Where was he looking for apartments?

"I can hook you up," Noah promised. "Just let me know, and we'll get you set up."

"I will have to keep that in mind." To my horror, Miles dropped into the chair next to mine. I looked to Valentina for help since that had been her chair before he showed up, but she didn't seem to mind. Instead, she sat across from me, smiling almost fondly as everybody satisfied their curiosity about our stepbrother.

I could have told them if only they would listen. This wasn't the real Miles. Only I had ever met the smirking, foul prick beneath the affable façade.

"We meet again." Miles settled back in his chair, stretching his long legs out in front of him.

"Where have you been tonight?" I asked, noting how different he looked from the rest of us. I had never seen any of our crew dressed like he was, similar to how I saw him at the penthouse. The curious glances and flat-out lusty gazes of passing girls made me nauseous.

"Around." Flashing a devilish grin, he added, "If you're so curious, I could take you along with me next time."

"You ride a motorcycle?" Lucian asked, leaning forward like his interest had been piqued. "What brand?"

"Harley-Davidson," Miles replied. "One of their new CVO Road Glide Limited models." I didn't know the first thing, but the odd reaction from Lucian and the other guys told me this was impressive for some reason.

"The one with the touchscreen and Bluetooth and everything? Shit, I would love to get a look at that." Noah almost sighed when he said it. Boys and their toys.

Sienna's head tipped to the side while her expression turned to one of disbelief. "I've never seen you look at me that way," she told him with a laugh, nudging him. "Little did I know you were cyclesexual."

"That's a new one," Noah said with a laugh, pulling her into his lap. It was good to see them this way. They had gotten close when she worked to revamp his image and saved his real estate empire. Their relationship was pretty young, only a handful of weeks, but they already teased each other like an old married couple. It made sense. We had all known each other all of our lives.

The outsider to the group didn't seem as though he was having any trouble fitting in. After a few minutes of pointless small talk, which I pointedly avoided getting pulled into, Miles stood. "Let me take the next round. What will everyone have?"

"More of the same," Valentina announced, holding up her wine glass. "They should have our orders in the system. And thank you," she called out as he backed away.

She then turned to me, and I really wished she didn't

have to look so superior. The girl was two minutes older, but she had a way of making it seem much longer when she put her mind to it. "See?" she asked. "It's not that hard to be friendly."

"He seems cool to me," Noah declared.

"He could read the back of a shampoo bottle, and I'd be riveted," Rose admitted, giving Colton a guilty little grin. "I've always been a sucker for British guys."

"Now she tells me," Colton groaned, also grinning.

Sienna draped an arm around his neck before rolling her eyes at me. "He's got a man crush, that's all."

"I would really love to get a look at that bike. Do you think you would mind if we asked to go out and see it?" Lucian asked.

I was going to bite my off tongue if this went on much longer. "Be right back," I announced, grabbing my purse and intending to head for the ladies' room. Anything for a minute to myself. All it took was a stupid motorcycle and a winning smile, and everybody was head over heels for him.

Once again, I asked myself if I was the problem. Why wouldn't anybody believe me when I told them I didn't trust him? I couldn't help but look over my shoulder on my way to the bathroom. There he was with a half-naked girl on either side of him, both of them tossing their hair and laughing. Yes, he was hot. I could admit that to myself, even if I would never dare admit it to my sister. But whatever happened to having a little dignity?

"Hey." I barely had the chance to recognize a man was speaking to me before he raised his voice. "I said hey! You with the red hair. Nice ass."

This was not the first time I had been cat-called at a bar. I didn't know a single woman who hadn't gone through this experience at least once. The best way to deal with it was always to ignore it, which is what I tried to do as I continued walking toward the back of the room. That was the last thing I needed, considering the mood I was in. The guy was lucky I was patient enough not to curse him out for everybody to hear.

"Why are you so fucking rude?" I felt his presence before his hand landed on my shoulder. Until then, I had not bothered looking his way, determined to pretend he didn't exist, but I couldn't exactly avoid him when he took hold of me and turned me around so we were face-to-face. He was tall, soft in an ex-athlete sort of way. Time and probably beer had added a layer of fat to what may have been muscle at one point.

And he was strong. The hand on my shoulder tightened menacingly. "Can't a guy give you a compliment, you frigid bitch," he demanded, leaning closer until the stench of beer almost choked me.

"Just leave me alone," I muttered, and instead of trying to pull away or throw his hand off, I let my knees go loose and ducked a few inches. He lost his grip, so I was free in a heartbeat and ready to shout for help from one of the guys.

"The fuck is your problem?" He reached for me again, this time gripping my wrist, and as much as I didn't want to give myself away, I yelped more in surprise than in pain.

"Oy!" A flash of black leather came from the corner of my eye before the stranger flew backward against the closest wall. It was almost like magic, the way he was there and then he wasn't.

There was no time to breathe when Miles pulled back a fist and slammed it against the guy's face. By now, everybody realized what was going on, and Colton quickly took hold of me and pulled me away from the fight. I couldn't pry my eyes from the sort of violence that would normally make me cringe and shudder. Miles hit the guy again in the face, making blood spurt from his nose before pummeling his ribs with rights and lefts.

That wasn't enough to end things, though. The stranger took him by his jacket and swung around, slamming Miles into the wall and landing a punch against his right cheek.

Dimly, almost in the back of my mind, I heard somebody shout something about calling the cops. Colton must have heard it, too, and he and Noah closed in on the brawling men. Miles managed to get one final shot that made my would-be attacker drop to the floor like a sack of potatoes. The fight was over. There was no question of who had won.

"We should go," Evan decided, approaching from behind me and giving my hand a firm tug which almost knocked me off my feet. I was swaying, dazed, as breathless as I would've been if I had been the one throwing punches. "Come on before Sienna has to take us all on as clients."

Evan had a point. This would cause all kinds of problems if it got out. As much as I wanted to go and leave this behind, it wouldn't have felt right to leave without Miles. He had only gotten into a fight because of me.

Before I knew what I was doing, I ran to where he leaned against the wall with a hand pressed to his wounded cheek. "Let's go. *Now*," I urged, tugging his jacket. "Before somebody calls the police."

He spat a mouthful of blood onto the floor before shooting one last dirty look at the man who was still unconscious. But he followed when I practically ran out of the bar behind everybody else. I was too humiliated to look at any of the whispering and pointing people we passed.

It felt like forever until we were outside again with everybody hanging around, wondering what to do.

"Looks like we'll have to continue this some other time." Miles looked my way before inclining his head toward a gleaming motorcycle parked half a block down. How he had managed to find parking in the middle of Manhattan was a mystery to me, but then so much about him was. "I'll get you home."

"Go ahead," Valentina urged, almost pushing me behind him. "I'll call you. Hurry."

What the hell was I doing? I had never been on a motorcycle before, much less with somebody I didn't trust. But he had fought for me, hadn't he? Maybe he just wanted to fight somebody, and that happened to be the most convenient option.

"Shouldn't I be wearing a helmet?" I asked once I was positioned behind him. Okay, so maybe it wasn't the worst thing in the world, with the smell of leather playing tricks on my senses while I slid my arms around his waist. Looking over his shoulder, I caught sight of his bloody knuckles as he took hold of the handlebars or whatever they were called.

"I'll be careful," he called out.

All of a sudden, there was a beast between my legs, and the vibrations were intense enough to make me squeal in surprise. It was a relief that the engine drowned out the sound, and I closed my eyes tight, bracing myself before we took off.

Once the strangeness wore off, it was a rush. Nothing between me and the wind blowing my hair back and making my loose, knee-length skirt flutter a little against my skin. We weren't going very fast. He kept his promise about being careful. But it was still enough to get my heart pumping.

And the buzzing between my legs didn't hurt either.

It wasn't until we reached my building's attached garage that the reality of what had just happened finally sank in. "We ran from the police," I announced as Miles rolled into an empty spot. My legs were shaking when I swung one of them over the seat to... dismount? Was that the right word for it?

"I don't know if I would be quite that dramatic." He was laughing but not in a cold or nasty way for once. "But we did escape before their arrival. And you had your first ride. What did you think?"

I thought I was insanely turned on. There wasn't a handheld vibrator in existence that could compete with that kind of power. "I think... you should wash that." I touched my fingers to my cheekbone before pointing to his. There was a cut there, and a bruise was beginning to take color. "Your knuckles too."

"Good thing there's running water upstairs." He was practically floating on air and in a better mood than I had seen him in yet. Was that all it took? Kicking the crap out of some jerk in a bar?

Once we were upstairs, the penthouse was dark and quiet, which was no surprise considering the late hour. I waved Miles on behind me. "There should be ointment in my medicine cabinet."

"You don't have to do this for me." Yet he followed me to the upper level where I knew there was a tube of Neosporin in my bathroom. I didn't think about it. I didn't plan it. Maybe somewhere in my subconscious, it seemed like the only thing to do. I had watched him knock somebody out for my sake. I could at least spare some antibiotic ointment.

"Nice room," he murmured behind me when we reached my suite, looking around the bedroom as I flipped the light switch.

"They didn't change much when I left for college." That was my way of explaining the teenage photos still sitting on my childhood dresser. There was no reason for me to get rid of them now. If anything, they made me smile when I looked at them, even as I tried to remember the version of me who existed ten years ago. Back before I knew I had a stepbrother.

"I imagined you and Valentina sharing a room, but then I suppose there was no need for that."

"Oh, God." I flipped on the bathroom light and opened the medicine cabinet over the vanity. "I could never share a room with her. For somebody so organized when it comes to her schedule, she is the most disorganized person in every other way."

"I thought twins were supposed to be alike."

"Wash your hands," I ordered rather than get into personal twin business he didn't deserve to know about. "And your face."

"Yes, ma'am." I forced myself to ignore his sarcasm, remembering how scared I was when that guy had taken me. There wasn't a doubt in my mind that one of my cousins would have jumped in if they realized what was happening. But they hadn't. Miles had. Miles who was not related to me by blood, had gotten nothing from me but negativity to this point. He had jumped in without waiting to be told, without asking questions.

"Does it hurt?" I asked, squeezing some of the ointment onto my finger and reaching up to dab it on his cut. Why was I doing it? He could've done it himself. Was I stupid enough to feel all protective of him now? I couldn't be. Still, there was nothing wrong with being human toward somebody else. I could put everything else aside for tonight.

"This is nothing compared to some of the scrapes I've

gotten into," he assured me, one corner of his mouth pulling up in a smirk. "You should've known me in my younger days."

"You do seem like somebody who could handle himself in just about anything," I admitted.

"That sounded suspiciously close to a compliment, you realize." His eyes twinkled when I risked looking into them. "You may want to be careful, or I might suspect you're becoming fond of me."

"Don't ruin it." But I was grinning when I looked up from his knuckles, now shining with a fresh layer of ointment. He was grinning back when our eyes locked, and someone stole all the air from the room. The gold seemed more prevalent for some reason, standing out against the green. Maybe it was the lighting. Maybe it was the three glasses of wine I drank, not to mention the whole fight thing. Nobody ever told me that could be an aphrodisiac.

"You're a little windblown." He reached out, brushing his fingers through my hair like he was trying to tame it after a ride with no helmet. "You'll have to tie your hair back the next time we take a ride."

Fighting to ignore the tingling of my skin, I whispered, "Who says there's going to be a next time?"

Snorting softly, he replied, "You should've seen your face when we got here. Wait and see. I'll have you wrapped around me again." There was barely a chance for me to process that before he added, "On the bike, of course." Right. Which meant there was no reason for my insides to go all hot or my heart to take off like a speeding train. No reason for the warmth of his breath fanning across my face to leave me fighting the impulse to lean in and find out what his generous mouth tasted like.

"Or now..."

Before I could pull myself back from the brink of an abyss, he pressed a hand to the small of my back and brought my body against his. I was still reeling from his sudden move when his mouth found mine, and a shock wave rolled through me. Pure heat, sizzling, searing my skin, and setting my mind on fire.

Stop this. I knew I had to. This was bad, and it couldn't happen. He was my freaking stepbrother and wrong for me in every conceivable way.

My body didn't think so, especially not when leaning against the vanity. He parted his thick thighs and pulled me closer while his tongue slowly stroked mine. He kissed me deeply and thoroughly like a man with all the time in the world and nothing better to do while the hand against my back slid south until he cupped my ass. Too good. I was powerless, completely under his spell, with no hope of resisting.

I didn't want to resist.

My pussy was wet and throbbing by the time I broke the kiss to come up for air. His lips moved over my jaw and down my throat while his soft grunts filled my ears. I let myself test the softness of his curls, lust flaring hotter at the sound of his helpless groans. Something big and hard pressed against my lower belly, and I could imagine myself rubbing my body against it to make him groan again. I could imagine a lot of things, starting right here against the vanity before moving to the bed.

Which was a serious problem.

What the hell was I thinking? My eyes flew open, and dread flooded my heart, dousing the flames that had been licking at my self-control only seconds ago. "You should be fine now," I told him in a breathless whisper, breaking away from his embrace like he was on fire. He may as well have been. I knew I would certainly get burned if I stayed too close for too long.

He didn't seem surprised. A little regretful, maybe, but that probably had more to do with the erection jutting out from his jeans. "Whatever you say," he murmured, a little breathless as he ran his hands through his hair to smooth down what I had tangled.

"And thank you," I added because it seemed like the right thing to say.

"Hey," he murmured, examining his knuckles, then looking at me with that same funny little smirk. "You're my *stepsister,* right?"

I didn't know what to say about that, so I settled for stepping aside and letting him walk past me through the bedroom. Somehow, I managed to wait until he was out the door before clasping my hands over my head and closing my eyes. I was caught between anger at myself and that weird, warm sense of gratitude that almost made me do something extremely stupid not half a minute ago.

I had come within moments of saying *fuck it* and giving in to the weakness I had for him. Disgusting. Stupid. Shameful, so long as I was being honest with myself.

A faint buzzing sound caught my attention. My phone was in my purse, tossed on the bed. I assumed it was Valentina checking to make sure I got home all right. If it wasn't, I resolved to text her to let her know I was safe.

It was Valentina, but she wasn't speaking only to me. "A group text?" I whispered, scrolling through the dozens of messages that had already been exchanged in the past twenty minutes.

Evan: *That was pretty badass back there!*
Noah: *Aria, what was it like on his bike?*

Colton: *Yeah, and don't spare any details. That bike is fucking gorgeous.*

Lucian: *I'm fucking burning with jealousy. Aria got to ride it? She doesn't even give a shit!*

Valentina: *Uh, the point was to see how Aria is doing and whether they got back to the penthouse okay.*

Sienna: *That accent! Sorry, but I can't get over it. Add whisking Aria off on his motorcycle, and he's like James Bond.*

Noah: *Sienna, do I need to be worried?*

Sienna: *I was going to ask you the same thing…*

Rose: *You can't still hate him, right, Aria?*

Son of a bitch. Now he was everybody's hero. Knowing these guys, they would dine out on that story for ages—how Miles had kicked the crap out of a guy for getting handsy with me.

With a sinking heart, I flopped face-first onto the bed before grabbing a pillow and screaming into it. Somehow, he had found a way to make everybody love him. And I hated him more than ever for it because there was a second where I had sort of felt the same way.

6

MILES

"Don't worry about a thing. I told you I had it all worked out. All you need to do is keep recovering." Checking myself out in the mirror over the dresser, I smirked at my reflection. "Your bills have been paid, and I wired an extra generous amount directly into your checking account. It's the least I could do."

The man currently overseeing the setup of my new offices sucked in what sounded like a pained breath on the other end of the call as if his broken ribs were bothering him. "Thanks, but did you have to hit me so hard? I could've played it up."

"How did I know you would have made it look legitimate?" I asked. It seemed like a reasonable question.

"You hired me to get shit done for you," he grumbled. "Not to get my ass kicked. You said I was only supposed to come on strong with the girl. Not that you were going to—"

He was boring me. "At any rate, it's over now," I reminded him, raising my voice to cut his off. "And you are substantially better off than you were before. Thank you again for your assistance."

"I only hope it was worth it," he muttered, ending the call. Stupid prick, as if I did anything that wasn't worthwhile.

I had gambled, and it had worked. I'd known Aria's family and friend group would be no match for a little violent chivalry. Something told me there weren't any fighters among them. At the most, they may have sparred at the gym, if that. Never had any of them engaged in a real brawl. They had no need to. There was always someone to do their fighting for them.

Everything was going according to plan. Even Aria, the original ice princess herself, had thawed considerably. There was none of that open hostility anymore, though I wouldn't have called us close by any means. It was progress, which was all that mattered. She would be putty in my hands before much longer.

I could have taken her that night. Then and there on the bathroom vanity if I'd felt like it. She wouldn't have put up a fight. That wasn't the problem. The problem was how much I'd genuinely wanted to. Not out of spite or with her greedy asshole of a father in mind, but simply because she was beautiful and the sheer joy shining from that beautiful face once I'd parked the motorcycle had revealed more about her than a thousand words could. The same wild, unspeakable joy had torn through me during my first ride and left me feeling euphoric. Unstoppable.

For that brief moment, we were the same. After a lifetime spent feeling separate, less than, even ashamed, I was understood.

Yet before I could make a terrible mistake, she'd put a stop to everything. For once, her mistrust had served me well. When I decided to claim Aria's fit young body, it would be on my terms, not the result of some foolish rush of hormones. I would make her want me. She would beg for my touch. Before long, she'd beg for my love as well.

Then, my stepfather and his lovely family would find out what it meant to suffer. What heartbreak and betrayal truly meant. I wouldn't stop at Aria, either. She was merely the tip of the iceberg.

One step at a time, however. I couldn't afford to jump ahead. Didn't they always say the joy was in the journey rather than the destination? So far, I had gotten quite a bit of enjoyment out of toying with them. It had been nearly a week and a half since I'd first moved into the penthouse, and though I was still bored senseless by these dull people, the pleasure of gaining their trust and esteem was immeasurable.

I brushed a piece of lint away from my shoulder, and something about the nearly surreal softness of the cable knit sweater stirred up a memory. Mom had been so proud of the fine wool sweater she'd somehow gotten her hands on as a Christmas gift for me. Years later, I figured she'd found it at some donation center. There was no way she could have afforded anything so well-made.

Back then, at that age and place in my life, I could never have conceived of owning a soft, expensive sweater such as this but a closet full of them. It meant I could appreciate what I had. How could Aria or Valentina or anyone in their circle? Luxury, excess, it was all they had ever known. I could almost feel sorry for them when I thought about things that way.

But my empathy only stretched so far. I squared my shoulders and strode into the hall, following the sounds of voices in the kitchen.

"I'm just saying you need to have Ari send a stylist over with something fantastic." I rounded the doorway as

Valentina finished making her proclamation. She stood near the stove, munching a slice of cucumber while Evelyn plated a roast and Aria spooned browned, steaming potatoes into a bowl. I hadn't expected them to be the ones doing the cooking. Didn't they have a staff? I'd seen their housekeeper several times, so I knew Evelyn didn't take all of the household work on her shoulders.

"Would you tell her, please?" Upon noticing me, Valentina gestured toward her mother with the uneaten bit of cucumber in her hand. "They're having this big party for her nonprofit, and she needs to look like a queen. She deserves it too. But she doesn't want to take advantage of a friendship or whatever by getting somebody we've literally known all of our lives to send a couple of gowns over for her to try on."

Through all this, Aria pointedly avoided looking my way but laughed softly at her sister's exasperation. "You changed your hair," I realized, admiring her now amethyst locks from across the room. She wore them in lustrous waves over her shoulders and down her back.

Aria's head snapped up, one hand touching her hair as if she was self-conscious. "I went to the salon today. It was time for something new." Her eyes briefly met mine before darting away while she attempted to hide a pleased little smile by ducking her head.

I then realized Valentina was still waiting for me to back her up. "I have to agree," I told Evelyn, reminding myself as I did how crucial it was to conceal my absolute loathing of the woman. There was no excuse for what she had done. She knew Magnus was married when she sank her claws into him. It took two to tango, certainly, and I would never have absolved Magnus from blame, but she played a part as well.

She laughed warmly, shaking her head. "How would

that look?" she countered, setting the roast aside before going to the glass door refrigerator and pulling a large salad from inside. "The women we help can't afford couture from Farrah Goldsmith."

"It's a special occasion. Thirty years, Mom." There was obvious pride ringing in Aria's voice and shining in her blue eyes when she looked at her mother. I had never seen such plain hero worship up close. "Everybody expects you to look exquisite, and you know Ari would love to help."

"I'll think about it," Evelyn murmured in a way that told me she was convinced. Her daughters had talked to her into it. All of her false modesty made me sick to my stomach. Yes, she had done good things for people who deserved it. But my mother had deserved it. She had deserved better than what life gave her at the hands of Evelyn Black.

"I've been salivating over the aroma of this roast." Magnus's booming voice preceded him, and soon he joined us in the kitchen. "Miles. I'm so glad you're joining us tonight. It will be nice to have all three of you here at once."

Aria's jaw clenched as she passed on her way to the dining room. She was still determined to resent me, though something made her hide it better than she had before. Was it gratitude after the fight at the bar or because of the kiss she couldn't resist? Either way, she hated me for it and likely hated herself for revealing her weakness the instant I touched her.

When I did have her, and I would, there was no doubt in my mind that it would help not to have to force myself to get it up. But it would be a job like any other. Another step along the path I had laid for myself. Which was why it could not come as the result of a rush of hormones. I needed to get a hold of myself before everything went to shit over a pair of great tits and a smart mouth I would love to fill with my cock.

"Let me help me with that." I took the salad bowl for Evelyn, forcing a smile, chatting with Magnus about his interest in AI and what it could mean for the future. This, I could handle. Aside from my mother, we had business in common.

"I would love to get in on the work you're doing." He took his seat at the head of the table, spanning a long, formal dining room. It seemed wasteful, all that space for so few people, to say nothing of the fine china and crystal at each place setting, the heavy silk tablecloth and napkins embroidered with the letter M for Miller.

I had once dreamed of living life at this level. Now, all I saw was the waste in the way he chose to live.

"Could we not talk about business tonight?" Evelyn planted a soft kiss against her husband's cheek before taking her seat at his right hand. Valentina sat at her right, leaving Aria to sit at Magnus's left. I gladly took the chair beside her, pretending not to notice how she stiffened at my nearness.

"Seriously, Dad." It was clear to me, at least, that she went out of her way to engage him while ignoring me. "Isn't it bad enough you've been having all your little hushed phone calls in your study night and day? Now you have to bring it to the dinner table." She shook her head, clicking her tongue.

Evelyn exchanged a glance with her husband before interjecting, "Now, you know it's my prerogative to chide your dad over working too hard, Aria."

"It's a habit," Magnus reminded his wife, chuckling. "I'll try to behave myself." The look they exchanged spoke volumes.

Volumes that were not lost upon their daughters. "Ugh."

Valentina dramatically rolled her eyes. "Do you two have to flirt in front of us? Don't get me wrong. I'm glad you, like, still enjoy each other…"

"Can you not say it *that* way?" Aria asked, looking pained. "I know we're adults, but yuck." Their parents laughed, telling me they got a great deal of enjoyment out of embarrassing their daughters. Some things were universal, no matter how much wealth a person amassed.

Somehow, I managed to look pleasant between bites of succulent roast beef. Evelyn could cook. I could give her that much. What a shame the juicy meat soured in my mouth as the happy couple gazed lovingly at each other.

That should have been my mother. I should have been at this table all these years. Instead, I was at the mercy of countless boyfriends, acquaintances, the men my mother gravitated toward in a desperate search for some semblance of normalcy and security. I couldn't imagine the life she once lived here in this city, though she had gone out of her way to describe it so many times. How fast-paced and colorful it was—all of her many friends and the travels she was able to enjoy while working as a model. Childbirth had gone a long way toward putting an end to her career, yet another layer of guilt that I'd grappled with in my youth. She used to sit at night with a bottle of vodka and a large book filled with photos from her younger days. So beautiful, so young. So undeserving of the shit Magnus had heaped upon her.

My hand tightened around my knife while everyone continued their mindless chatter. These girls didn't know what it meant to hold the hand of the only person they've ever loved as they took their final, painful breath after years of suffering. They couldn't conceive of the pain of watching a parent deteriorate before their very eyes. The beautiful, spirited girl from those photo shoots may as well have been a ghost the way my mother now was.

"Excuse me." It was the first thing I'd said since we sat. All eyes turned toward me, watching as I pushed my chair away from the table and stood. "I forgot to place a call to one of my advisors, and it can't wait until tomorrow. I won't be long." It came out in a rush, punctuated by dropping my napkin onto the chair. I needed air. I needed quiet. My thoughts were spiraling, memories overlapping, bitterness gripping my very soul.

I headed straight for the balcony leading out from the front room and all but threw myself out there, taking one grateful gulp after another of air that had gone cold now that the sun had set. The city was coming alive beneath me, all those many floors below. Was this how God felt, if there was a god? Looking down over creation, observing the lights and the activity without being part of it?

I pulled out my phone, though not with the purpose of placing a call. I didn't often pull up the private folder in my photo app, but it was at moments like this when a visual reminder of everything I'd lost came in handy. I had saved photos over the years, transferring them from one device to the next. It was the ones of my mother and me which I held most dear.

She was healthy once when her demons hadn't yet taken hold of her. Smiling on Christmas Day, presenting me with a bicycle was the last good Christmas I could remember when she had a steady job. Everything had begun to unravel following that when she met the man who first enticed her to try a drug that would help her forget her worries. Little had she known, her worries would only explode after that point.

She never knew the kind of comfort, warmth, and love

now surrounding me. Why couldn't she have been happy? Why did every aspect of her life need to be a struggle?

"Promise me." Fuck, her voice had been so weak by then, ravaged by years of heavy drinking, weakened by the drugs that had flowed throughout her body. All of the money I'd made wasn't enough to save her. With the best hospitals and rehab centers and top doctors, the damage had already been done. *"Promise me you will take care of yourself when I'm gone."*

Standing on that balcony with the wind stirring my hair and stinging my cheeks, I could almost feel her frail hand in mine. I could smell the hospice and hear the steady, incessant beeping of machines.

And in my head, I heard my vow, one I had been glad to make. *"I promise I will, and I promise I am going to make them pay for ever hurting you. All of them. They are going to know what they've done, and they will regret it for the rest of their lives. I swear, Mom. I'm going to hurt them."*

Then she had smiled, and it had been so long since I had seen her smile. For the first time since she began to fall apart, she looked happy and at peace. I needed to believe she died that way.

"Hey. Are you okay out here?"

I scrambled to compose myself at the sound of Aria's soft voice behind me. Of all times for her to come sneaking around. "Just wrapped up my call," I announced over my shoulder, gazing out into the night.

It should have been me.

Her life should have been mine.

"I was running up to my room to grab a sweater, and I saw you out here. You looked..." Obviously, kindness was not her forte. It was like she had lost track of what she wanted to say, eventually going silent.

"I'm fine."

She came closer, footsteps ringing out against the steel beneath our feet. "I got the feeling you were having a rough time back there in the dining room."

"You're very perceptive." Shit, I couldn't afford to let the bitterness leak out.

If anything, she seemed to appreciate that, laughing gently before reaching my side and gripping the iron railing running in front of us. "I hope everybody hasn't come on too strong. You know what I mean. With Dad making this big deal about including you in the family and everybody trying to meet and learn about you, it must be a lot."

Good. Let her think that was the problem. "You have a nice relationship with your parents," I observed, staring outward rather than looking at her. There was no hope of concealing my rancor if I were looking her in the eye. She would see through me.

"I know I'm lucky. I know lots of people who don't and never did. I don't take it for granted." That would probably be a first. I couldn't imagine how she didn't take her life for granted. It seemed an impossibility growing up this way, surrounded by priceless artwork and drinking from Baccarat crystal with an entire city laid out before her.

She stretched her arms to the sides, sighing and gripping the railing tighter. "It probably seems like we've had it easy," she mused, almost as if she read my mind. "And I guess we have in so many ways. But Mom raised my sister and me a lot differently than other people our age in our circle. She grew up like a normal person. She went through... a lot," she added, her voice cracking. "The sort of stuff she won't even tell us. My Uncle Barrett has made vague references to it from time to time, and he's always furious and bitter when he does. And usually kind of tipsy," she added with a snicker.

"Alcohol does tend to loosen tongues," I agreed. Hence, the fact that I'd greatly lessened my intake since moving in with the family.

"I'm sure you went through a lot. You worked your way up from nothing." Was that genuine respect in her voice? Or did she feel sorry for me? "And now you can start fresh out here... with a new family."

"Don't pretend that doesn't make you sick," I warned.

Her laughter was soft, a note of wry understanding running beneath it. "I won't."

"I'm not going to forget her."

"You shouldn't forget her," she replied. "Nobody would expect you to do that. She was your mom. She'll always be your mom."

Her empty reassurances left a bitter taste in my mouth. I swallowed it back, keen to take advantage of her sympathy. "I miss her," I choked out and was rewarded by her sympathetic sigh.

"I'm sorry. I really am."

The strangest thing happened. She touched my shoulder, her hand molding around the muscle, fingers pressing in. "But, you know, everybody around here likes you and wants you to be part of things. I'm pretty sure Lucian wants to get into a serious relationship with your motorcycle."

I didn't expect to laugh, much less loud and hard the way I did. Her unexpected comment was refreshing. She had a sense of humor under that prickly, bitchy veneer. "It'll be a cold day in hell," I told her, making her laugh again.

I took the risk of looking her way, finally meeting her gaze. Her eyes sparkled like sapphires in the lights from the countless skyscrapers surrounding us, emanating warmth that didn't seem entirely forced. She offered a genuine if slightly awkward, smile. "Come on. Let's go in and finish eating. Valentina swung by Baked and picked up their apple pie. It's the best in the world, I swear. There won't be any left if we don't hurry."

Something about the moment left me wanting to draw it out. We had crossed a threshold. Returning to the dining table would end the tentative closeness we'd achieved.

"Thank you." I covered her hand with mine. "You have no idea how much it means. It's kind of you to reach out."

Her lashes fluttered, confusion passing over her face before she replied, "Sure. You're welcome."

It was a risk, but what was life without it? She flinched slightly but didn't make a move to stop me as I opened my arms and slowly closed them around her. "Really," I murmured as she returned the hug. "Hearing that from you means everything. For some reason, your acceptance is what matters most. Probably because I started us out on the wrong foot."

"You sure as hell did." But she laughed softly and loosened up a little.

It wasn't bad holding her this way. The scent of berries lingered in her hair and tickled my nose when I turned my face closer to inhale the sweetness. It allowed me to loosen up as she had, to tighten my hold and savor the way her body fit against mine. "Why do you dye your hair so many different colors?" I asked.

She chuckled softly. "I don't know. I've never found it easy to stand out, I guess. This is one way I can do it." The poor girl had no idea how she stood out without trying and how her radiance, beauty, and sharp mind set her apart.

I couldn't recall the last time I'd received a hug purely for the sake of comfort, and this one came from a girl who had all but vowed to hate me forever. There was something satisfying in it enough to make me want more.

When I pulled my head back, she did the same, leaving us gazing into each other's eyes. Searching. Questioning. When her mouth parted, the sight of her tempting lips left me ready to abandon my plans and throw caution to the wind. One more kiss. What harm could it do?

"Uh... guys. Were you planning on coming back in at some point?" Valentina stood at the half-open door, wrapping her arms around herself when a stiff breeze blew past. "Everything okay?" she asked, regarding us almost warily.

"Everything's fine." Aria wasted no time hurrying inside. Standing behind her, I caught the look her twin wore as she brushed past. The look someone wore when there would be a conversation later. One in which Aria would have to explain her change of heart, which would make her think about me long after we'd parted ways for the evening. The girl was officially off-balance when it came to me and her opinion thereof.

I ducked my head on my way inside to conceal the glee sizzling through me like lightning. So far, I'd managed to turn every situation to my advantage. I would have to seal my latest victory with a large slab of apple pie.

Though I doubted it would be any sweeter than the lips I'd come so close to tasting once again.

I needed to be more cautious. My attraction to her could not play a part in what had to be done. Otherwise, I'd do well to give up, and that wasn't going to happen.

7

ARIA

"Heads up! We'll be landing soon. Here you go." Valentina tapped on her phone before shining her proud smile on all of us. "Your itineraries have been delivered to your devices."

Like magic, my phone buzzed, and I reached for it the way everybody else reached for theirs. She was nothing if not organized and maybe a little bossy, not that I minded. When it came time to get eight people together for a three-day weekend, a little organization came in handy, especially this group, with their strong personalities and vastly different opinions on just about everything. Only the fact that we had known each other our entire lives made it possible for us to get along sometimes. We had learned to accept each other's personality quirks.

Like Lucian, who poured himself a healthy slug of vodka before topping it off with a minuscule amount of Bloody Mary mix. He then opened the cap on a bottle of Tabasco and added a few extra shakes to his drink. "Whatever happened to taking it easy on a weekend off?" he teased Valentina, who stuck her tongue out at him.

"You might want to slow down on those," Evan advised from his seat, eyeing Lucian. "I thought you said you wanted to hit the slopes first thing."

"And look." Colton tapped his phone and held it up for all to see. "Our amazing Valentina even scheduled in time for us to ski this morning."

"Shove it up your ass, Colton," she muttered, which filled the jet with laughter. "These are suggestions. Stay in bed all weekend if that's what you have in mind. Those who want to ski will head up the road to the lodge."

"I know that's what I'll be doing," I announced. I could hardly wait. When it came to most things, I used caution. I didn't like to drive fast and never swam out into deep water at the beach. I was not a daredevil. Maybe that was what made skiing such a thrill—the rush, speed, and sense of taming the laws of physics.

"Some of us were looking forward to spending a little time off the slopes." Sienna gave me a meaningful look, cuddling up next to Noah.

I wasn't jealous. That much I knew for sure. There was nothing I wanted more for the people I loved than their happiness, and Sienna was clearly beyond happy with Noah. Meanwhile, he walked around looking like a man who had accidentally hit the lottery. I was glad for them. That didn't mean I wouldn't have liked somebody to cuddle with.

"Feel free to join us, but you don't have to," Valentina announced with a roll of her eyes. "Honestly. It's like trying to herd cats."

Rose approached her from behind and threw her arms around my sister's neck. "We appreciate you," she assured her, placing a big, smacking kiss against her cheek. "Thank you for putting this together." She then shot the rest of the jet a very meaningful sort of look, like a warning.

"Of course," Noah quickly agreed. "This was your idea, and it was a damn good one. Thank you, Valentina," he added in an almost sickly sweet voice.

"Fuck off," she retorted, laughing. There was no hanging out with this group of guys without developing a thick skin. It was pretty much necessary.

I settled back in my seat, closing my eyes and exhaling slowly. Was it possible to consciously release tension? I was sure as hell trying my best. I had been carrying way too much of it in my shoulders and neck lately.

If I felt like looking back at the timeline and piecing things together, which I definitely did not, I would come to a pretty obvious conclusion. I had woken up with a tension headache the day after dinner with Miles, and two days later, it still slightly throbbed. I hated thinking about him while we were so far from the city, minutes away from landing on the private airstrip ten miles from the cabin that had been in our family since we were around eight years old. The cabin in Vail owned by Colton's parents was where we used to spend Christmas, but this cabin was perfect for a quick weekend getaway. Homier too.

I craved the clean air and the sting of the wind on my cheeks. As much as I loved living in Manhattan, there were times when a girl needed to be able to hear herself think.

On landing, Valentina peered through the window closest to her chair. "Awesome. They're already waiting." She pointed to the four black SUVs she had rented for the weekend. "I figured couples could have their own car. Evan and Lucian, you'll be sharing, and I'll share with Aria. Just to get us back and forth to the lodge or if we want to drive down to the village from the cabin."

"You thought of everything." Evan sounded appreciative without a hint of snark, rubbing Valentina's shoulder on the way past once we began to disembark. "We all owe you one."

"Please," my sister laughed, gathering her things before pulling on her coat. "If I started counting all the favors I'm owed, I would never stop."

The first breath of crystal clear, cold air upon stepping out onto the staircase was heavenly. I filled my lungs and smiled, tipping my head back to soak in the brilliant sunshine before heading to one of the vehicles. The jet crew started unloading our bags while Colton and Noah advised them which vehicles to load things into. Not that it mattered since we were all going to the same place. They needed to feel like they were an important part of the trip.

The purring of an engine caught my attention halfway across the tarmac. The sound got louder as the plane approached. It was a small plane, one of those single-engine jobs. Sienna and Rose stopped to watch, too, the three of us following the plane's approach until it touched down at the other end of the strip and began rolling our way.

It was only when the window to the pilot's left opened, and a familiar face appeared that my insides went cold, and my stomach dropped like a rock. *Miles*. What the hell was this? He waved before shutting down the plane, leaving nothing but silence once the propeller went still.

A fucking pilot... damn, that's hot.

"What the hell is he doing here?" I whispered to my sister, who seemed unbothered.

"What?" She turned, a hand over her eyes to shield them from the sun. "Oh. I don't know. I guess one of the guys asked him to come along."

A likely story. She had planned every aspect of this trip,

and I was supposed to believe she was cool with an unexpected guest? "Are you serious?" I whispered.

Who invited him?

Who was I going to have to kill?

"What's the problem? I thought you two were so friendly now." I was glad for my sunglasses since they concealed how I rolled my eyes at her remark. She would not let me live it down. It was a simple hug. I felt sorry for him. He lost his mom. He was obviously feeling sad.

He'd managed to humanize himself. And all because I responded to him like a human being, it meant I deserved ridiculed.

"There he is!" Jogging down the stairs from the jet, Lucian raised a hand in Miles's direction. Evan followed close behind him with the two of them helping unload baggage from the small plane.

"I should've known," I muttered, reminding myself to smack their heads together the first time I got the chance. They were formidable men. They had their shit together. All it took was a new friend with flashy toys to turn them into middle schoolers. "And they deliberately didn't say anything the whole way up here because they knew I'd be annoyed."

"Lighten up," Valentina advised once our bags were loaded into the rear of the SUV. "You know there's plenty of room in the cabin for all of us. Don't ruin your weekend by being so negative."

"I am not—" I cut myself off because, in all honesty, I *was* being negative. "I don't like surprises," I amended, which was the truth.

"Point taken. Now, let's remember we're adults, and we came up here to have a good time." She slapped my ass on the way past, opening the driver's side door and hopping behind the wheel. "Oh, and I'm driving."

As we pulled away, Miles and I exchanged a glance. He was loading his things into the SUV Lucian and Evan would be using. The windows were tinted, so there was no reason for him to know I was looking at him. Yet, for some reason, his smile widened as he watched us pass.

I stewed silently the entire way to the cabin. To think I had been looking forward to this weekend. I could see the rest of our time in Vermont spread out in front of me. Instead of relaxing and enjoying myself with my friends, I would always have one eye on him. I couldn't explain it. I had this driving need to watch him like a hawk. He hadn't done anything openly untrustworthy or harmful to this point. As much as Valentina's snarky comments set my teeth on edge, she was right. We had seemed to cross a threshold together back at the apartment a few days ago.

Why couldn't I get rid of the nagging feeling in the back of my mind? It didn't matter how I tried to push it aside and forget it or how many times I told myself to get along with him for Dad's sake. It meant so much that we got along and became a family.

None of that was enough to cool off the rush of boiling heat that bubbled up in me like lava about to explode from a volcano when I realized Miles was inside that little plane. Nothing about my reaction made sense on the surface. Why couldn't I get over my initial feelings and move on? Life would be so much easier if I could.

Before long, the cabin loomed up ahead. "There she is," Valentina announced. Her voice was light and happy. She didn't carry the burden of mixed feelings the way I did. She could look at our family cabin and see nothing but happy memories while I asked myself what gave Miles the right to think he could swoop in and be part of our new memories. I was acting no better than a spoiled brat, wasn't I? Maybe a few runs down the slopes would clear my head. It always did.

I was glad to be one of the first to arrive. It gave me the chance to step inside and absorb the place in peace. The two-story main room spread out almost immediately when I stepped through the front door. The fireplace and its towering chimney were flanked by a pair of enormous windows overlooking the Green Mountains in the near distance. Snow-frosted trees against a brilliant blue sky made my heart swell. I couldn't explain the connection to this cabin. I could only drink in the rich, warm woods and smooth stones comprising the hearth and the chimney above it. I ran my hands over them the way I had so many times before.

"Kitchen's stocked!" Valentina announced, heading straight for it. That was one of the more recent renovations, with my Aunt Lourde redesigning the room to update it considerably. The forest green cabinets and copper fixtures meshed well with the earthy color scheme.

"The liquor cabinet too," I confirmed, checking. We had used the same caretaking service for years, and they had never been anything less than accommodating when it came to making sure we had everything we needed no matter how many people would be staying.

"Where are you going?" Valentina called out once I started up the wide, wooden staircase with a bag slung over my shoulder and a wheeled suitcase in one hand.

"Where do you think?' I asked as I climbed. "I'm going to my room to unpack."

"What's your hurry? At least wait until everybody gets here."

"Everybody knows their way around by now. I don't need to give a tour." And I didn't need to run into Miles. Not yet. I wasn't prepared to spend the weekend with him. I didn't want him to take the moment we had a few nights ago and make more out of it than there was. I didn't want him acting all weird because I'd let him hug me.

I especially didn't want to remember how nice that brief hug had felt. And how disappointed I'd been when Valentina interrupted us. She had barely stopped giving me shit about it, and now I would have to be in Miles's presence without the distraction of work to separate us. She would be watching closely. It was one of those twin things. I knew exactly how she thought.

When I started emptying my suitcase into the dresser, voices overlapped downstairs. As bossy as ever, Valentina directed everybody to their rooms, their heavy footsteps pounding up the stairs barely drowning out the laughter and excited chatter.

There was one distinctive voice I hadn't heard yet that stuck out from the rest. Maybe he was looking around, getting a feel for the place. Would it be hopelessly stupid to hang out in here until I was sure he had reached his room? If I had to ask the question, it meant I already knew the answer. I wouldn't be able to avoid him all weekend.

The most obvious answer was also the most logical. Pulling my new navy blue snowsuit from my duffel bag, I stripped off my turtleneck and jeans. We were supposed to go skiing according to Valentina's itinerary. It would give me an excuse to get out of here and, hopefully, away from somebody who was starting to bring to mind gum stuck to the bottom of my shoe. I couldn't get rid of him, and I wasn't entirely sure I wanted to.

Things had quieted down considerably by the time I finished suiting up, adding a pair of black, faux fur-lined boots to the outfit before cinching the belt around my waist.

Armed with my gloves and goggles, I stepped out of the room, hoping to sneak out to the lodge a couple of miles down the road until I was noticed.

Since when did my luck go that well?

He was the only one down there, standing in the center of the main room. His hands were clasped behind his back while he stared at the fireplace, sunlight playing off his blond curls. His back was to me as I observed him from the open passage running in front of four of the cabin's eight bedrooms and overlooking the main room. Stepping up to the railing running along its length, I held my breath, waiting to see what he would do next.

He took a deep breath, shoulders rising and falling before he released a sigh. All at once, he turned so suddenly I didn't have time to react when he found me standing there. Somehow, he didn't look surprised.

He did, however, look annoyed. Maybe even angry. Brows drawn together, his lips pulled into a tight line. I could practically hear him grinding his teeth from where I stood so many feet above him. For a second there, he was the same guy I first noticed at the spin studio. The one who had followed me around New York without a word, silently observing, maybe judging.

It faded in a blink like somebody dragging an eraser across a whiteboard to wipe it clean. I hadn't imagined it. I needed to keep the memory close to the forefront.

"I didn't imagine you were a ski freak," he called out, nearing the stairs. There was something almost menacing in his footfalls. I was making it up, I had to be. He wasn't a threat to me.

"Some say freak, some say enthusiast. I've been looking forward to getting out there for weeks."

I lifted my chin once he reached the top of the stairs,

looking ridiculously dashing in a knee-length black coat with a charcoal gray turtleneck underneath. He could have been posing for a magazine spread when he leaned against the railing, looking me up and down.

"Do you prefer the bunny slopes?" he taunted with a smirk, slowly taking in every inch of my suit. Damn the heat that spread through me everywhere his gaze landed. This wasn't that lava I was thinking of earlier, something that would decimate everything in its path. Yet somehow, it felt more dangerous.

"I left them behind years ago. How about you?" Folding my arms, I arched an eyebrow. "Don't tell me you're a champion skier as well as a licensed pilot."

"No championships as of yet," he allowed, lifting a shoulder. "But you never know. I was about to change up and hit the slopes with the guys myself. We can go together. I'll only be a minute." Whistling, he passed on the way to his room which was further down the hall, something that came as a relief.

Not that I thought he would try to sneak into my room during the night. Why would my thoughts stray in that direction?

I hardened my resolve a little more with every heavy step I took down to the first floor. So Evan and Lucian had invited him skiing too. I made a mental note to thank them personally for being so welcoming and not at all a complete thorn in my side.

8

MILES

One thing was for certain—standing at the top of one of the resort's intermediate slopes, the four of us abreast as we prepared for the first warm-up run of the day, Aria could fill out a ski suit. I could barely take my eyes off her long enough to be sure my goggles were secure. I had seen her in workout clothes, jeans, and skirts, but never had she worn something so completely form-fitting that showcased her firm body so perfectly that my hands ached to test her curves.

"See you down there!" Lucian took off, followed by Evan, the two of them expertly weaving their way down the snow-covered hillside. They'd probably been on skis from the time they could walk or soon after. I had spent the first twenty years of my life regarding skiing as the ultimate wealthy person's sport. Something spoiled rich people did while visiting their cabins and ski lodges.

Such as the one in which I would be spending the weekend. Yet another part of the life I could have and should have led.

"You ready?" Aria offered a cheeky grin before she shot

forward without warning. I couldn't be irritated with her head start when it was so pleasant gazing at her peach of an ass as she seemed to fly down the slope.

I started off behind her, keeping her in my sights. I had only been on skis since midway through my college days, a scholarship student surrounded by the wealthy who had first exposed me to a world I'd only ever imagined. It was a sport I'd taken to quite easily. Mom used to tell tales of trips she'd taken in her modeling days—Aspen, Switzerland, Italy. She had tasted this lifestyle and had it cruelly ripped from her.

I couldn't optimize my speed while obsessing over memories that were not even mine to begin with. Pushing them from my head, I focused on catching up to her, which I did roughly halfway down the course. She veered right, placing more distance between us, and a quick glance her way revealed what looked like laughter before she shot forward again. She had me beat. I didn't happily admit to defeat, but there was no denying it.

By the time I reached her, she was yawning, staring at her wrist as if checking the time. "Took you long enough." I didn't mind losing so much when I heard the obvious joy in her voice. If she could taunt me, she was growing more comfortable with me. I could lose a single race if it meant advancing in the much larger picture.

"That's the problem with racing a cheater who takes a head start," I pointed out, lifting my goggles and narrowing my eyes. "It means you have to work harder to catch up."

"Yeah, yeah. Tell me another good one. I let you catch up to me, didn't I?" Her saucy grin did things to me. Bad things I had no business imagining, such as taking her back to that palatial cabin and tying her to the bed. Stroking those amethyst locks of hers while her head bobbed in a quick, steady rhythm, lips wrapped around my cock. We would do that. We would do all of it, but it had to be on my terms. Lust couldn't have a damn thing to do with it, at least not on my end.

"You like to go fast, do you?" I asked, pursing my lips as I admired the way the navy fabric clung to her curves. If she were any other man's daughter, what I wouldn't have already done to her.

"Sure. What, do you want me to show you again how much I like it?" She eyed the slope we'd come down. "I could go for another run before we move on to something more challenging." Her brazen confidence softened something in me. Something warmer, something comfortable and familiar.

"I wouldn't pass up the opportunity for another race." I eyed the slope, then shrugged. "But I was thinking of something else. Later. What do you say?"

"I say..." Her head tipped to the side, skeptical. "I would like more information."

"Meet me on the front porch at midnight." With that, I continued toward where Lucian and Evan waited for the lift. I hadn't given her the chance to refuse and hadn't received confirmation she would join me, but I wasn't worried. She couldn't back down from a challenge, not from me.

∽

It was half past eleven, and the evening was winding down. Colton and Rose had escaped to their room an hour ago, maybe more. Sienna had given Noah a meaningful look, then sauntered up the stairs not long after. Before calling it a night, he stayed behind for another few hands of poker at the round table between the kitchen and main room. All the while, Aria read a book, curled up in a deep, overstuffed chair near the fire on the other side of the room. She twirled a strand of hair around one finger, deeply engrossed.

So engrossed, in fact, she hadn't done much more than stare at the same page for the last two hands. I was the only one who noticed or paid attention.

There wasn't a doubt in my mind she was questioning whether she ought to take me up on my challenge. She would ignore her distrust of me if only to show me up. That was fine. So long as she followed the trail of breadcrumbs I so carefully sprinkled for her.

"We could make this interesting." Evan grinned at me before turning to Valentina, currently scowling at her cards. "What do you say next hand, we try strip poker?"

In another life, I might have liked Valentina quite a bit. She pulled no punches and didn't give much of a shit whether anyone cared. Her face contorted in a mask of disgust before she retorted, "Dude, my cousin is playing with us. That's disgusting."

"And her stepbrother, don't forget," I quipped. Soft scoffing floated our way from Aria's side of the room, but she continued the pretense of reading. "Though you aren't cousins by blood, are you?" I pointed out.

"No, but he's our aunt and uncle's nephew by marriage," Valentina explained as she studied her cards. "It just makes sense to call him our cousin. We all practically shared a playpen when we were little. Either way, my clothes are staying where they are, thank you."

"Just an idea," Evan insisted. "Can't blame a guy for trying."

"Actually, you can." She squinted across the table at him, the two of them the only ones who hadn't folded. "What's it gonna be? I call. Show me what you've got."

"Two pairs. Jacks over nines." Smirking, he spread his cards on the table and reached for the chips.

That was until Valentina placed a trio of sevens on the table before pulling the chips her way. "And because I'm a gracious winner, that will be my last hand," she announced gleefully. "We'll settle up in the morning." She hummed happily to herself as she gathered her chips while Evan scowled, and I shared a laugh with Lucian.

"It's been a long day." Lucian stretched, groaning, then pushed back from the table. "I think I'll head up. Who's doing breakfast in the morning?"

"You mean brunch, I hope," Evan muttered, gathering a handful of empty beer bottles and taking them to the kitchen. "I'm not one of you early risers."

"Either way, Rose and Sienna are making pancakes," Valentina announced. "Aria and I will take breakfast on Sunday before we head out."

All through this, Aria maintained her silence. I went through the motions of tidying up, pushing the chairs in, and finishing my lager before tossing the empty bottle into a recycle bin. I had milked two bottles of beer all evening, intent on keeping a clear head.

"Are you coming up anytime soon?" Valentina called down from the second-floor passage overlooking the main room.

Aria looked up at her, shrugging. "I'm pretty content down here right now. But don't worry. I'll kill the fire when I come up." In the reflection from the large windows spanning either side of the chimney, I noticed when Valentina's gaze landed on me. She was reluctant to leave us alone, but it wasn't enough to stop her from retreating to her room. I waited until the door closed and again for another two doors to close upstairs before speaking to Aria for the first time in hours.

"It's not quite midnight," I pointed out in a low voice on my way to the kitchen. "But my offer still stands. Meet me on the porch."

"For what?" She snapped the book shut without bothering to use a bookmark, telling me exactly how much attention she had paid to a single word.

"Something I think you'll enjoy." I wasn't about to give her another hint, deciding instead to head straight for the hooks embedded in the wall to the left of the front door, where my coat waited. If she followed, I had won.

The solar lights lining both sides of the pathway leading from the porch stairs were striking against snow painted purple by the moon. Lights dotted the landscape in the distance, revealing the presence of cabins and lodges throughout the valley. It was a beautiful, peaceful scene, one whose value I could not help but notice despite my distracted, troubled thoughts.

Thoughts of the girl inside, most likely pacing as she fought herself. There was no pretending she didn't hold my attention. I'd played terribly all evening, too concerned with the way the fire defined her delicate profile. I asked myself what she was thinking and noted her chewing of her lip from time to time as if something worried her.

I didn't care. I couldn't. There was no room for it. I had made a vow.

With my back to the door, there was no need to conceal a triumphant grin when I heard the hinges squeak softly. "Okay, I'm here." She sounded like the brat she was, which made my smile widen. If nothing else, she was an amusing girl. Fun to play with.

"It's about time." I reached into my pocket and withdrew

a set of keys to one of the SUVs. "Come on. I have something to show you."

Her disparaging groan rang out when I turned away. "I've heard that line before, you know."

Trotting down the stairs, I retorted, "Yet you're still following me." She was, too, her feet crunching the gravel beneath us on our way to the cars.

"It had better be good, is all. I could be warm in bed right now."

"There's one thing you need to learn about me. I am *always* good." Turning toward her, I had a chance to notice her scowl or disapproval. "Lighten up," I advised, opening her door before rounding the vehicle to open my own.

She seemed to have taken a vow of silence along the drive down to the airstrip. Her fists were clenched in her lap, her right knee jiggling. That was what I did to her.

At this time of night, there was very little traffic, only a pair of vehicles passing in the other direction. Otherwise, the road was ours, illuminated by the moon and the SUV's lights. More than once, I caught a glimpse of eyes glowing in the darkness on either side, observing our progress. Wolves? Bears?

Aria noticed, too, shivering and rubbing her arms. "I'm pretty sure I saw a wolf."

She was sitting next to one, and I bit my tongue to keep a straight face. "I hope we don't break down on the side of the road."

"Don't even joke about that."

I was content to sink into silence over the last few minutes of our journey. "Why are we here?" she asked when our destination was clear.

My plane waited, fully fueled as I'd requested. Once I had noticed her scowling reaction to my arrival, there was no question of bringing her out with me if only to show off. However, after our time on the slopes, it was obvious she needed to be put in her place. We'd see how brave she was when it came to true speed.

And altitude.

"You want to go flying? At this time of night?" So it *was* possible to impress her or to at least elicit a reaction other than contempt. She was slow and hesitant climbing down from the SUV, but she followed me to the single-engine Cessna before looking my way with a mixture of intrigue and concern radiating from her eyes.

"Why not? This is as good a time as any. You haven't lived until you've seen the mountains from above, in the moonlight. It's breathtaking." Frowning, I added, "Unless you're afraid. We can go back now if it would make you feel better."

"Shut up. I'm not a child." Rolling her shoulders back, she tightened her jaw before taking a deep breath. "Okay. Let's go. This could be fun."

"It will be." I opened the door and held out a hand to help her inside, pretending to ignore the shiver that ran through her at my touch. It led me to assist in buckling her in, knowing the way her body betrayed her. She sucked in a breath while I took my time sliding the straps across her chest, one she didn't release until the buckle clicked, and I withdrew my hands.

Stand down, I warned myself as I rounded the plane's nose, then climbed in. We would never get off the ground if I didn't keep my dick in check. Somehow, I doubted attacking her in the cockpit would be anything but awkward.

"How long have you been flying?" Her voice was soft

now, awestruck as she looked over the instruments. It must have been entirely foreign.

"I got my license two years ago."

"What made you decide to do that?" she asked.

"The same thing that led me to motorcycling, skiing and sports cars. We haven't discussed my admiration for them yet, have we?" She shook her head as I finished running down the items on my checklist. "I like to go fast. And I like the option of going wherever I want to go, whenever I wish. It's freedom."

"I can understand that."

"But you've always had that ability, haven't you?" Fuck. I shouldn't have said that. It wouldn't do for her to know I'd been thinking as much as I had about the differences in our upbringing.

Instead of firing back some smart-ass comment, she seemed to take my statement seriously. "You're right. I've had the privilege all my life. I'm glad you have that freedom now."

My chest warmed at the sincerity pouring from her voice, reminding me of what I'd gone without for most of my life—being understood and *seen*. I had no idea how much I'd missed it until now.

Good sense pulled me up short before I could forget what this was all about. Why did she have to be so fucking empathetic? Was it sincere or merely lip service?

It was best to let it go. "All right. Prepare yourself."

Her laughter was tight, half-hearted. "You're the one who needs to be prepared, pilot." She wasn't wrong. I was prepared, so it took very little time for us to taxi down the runway and lift off the tarmac.

Her strangled squeal took me by surprise. "With that

private jet sitting there, you're not used to taking off?" I asked with a laugh.

"This is different!" she shouted over the engine and propeller. "This is... this is amazing!" The sheer joy in her voice brought an unexpected smile to my face as we climbed closer to the moon.

"Wow." When I looked her way, I found her touching the backs of her fingers to the corners of her eyes. She was crying. I didn't need to ask why. I'd felt the same rush of almost crushing emotion the first time I took off in a small plane like this one. Feeling so close to the world outside and the wind currents passing around the plane's body, I wanted to reach out and grab a handful of stars. The illusion was there, brought on by an enormous moon that looked close enough to touch.

"What do you think?" I asked as we rounded the resort we'd skied earlier. "Can you see the cabin from here?"

"I can't quite tell." She craned her neck, looking through the window on her side in search of the dark green roof.

"Let me help you." I banked right, making her squeal again as the plane tilted on her side. "Can you see it now?" I chuckled over her panicked gasps for breath.

"Don't do that!" she barked. "Jesus, are you trying to give me a heart attack?"

"Not quite yet."

She took a beat before muttering, "What does that mean?"

I leveled the plane again before flipping a switch, opening power to the yoke on her side of the cockpit. "I am saying you are going to fly the plane now."

"Fuck off."

I couldn't help but burst out laughing at her deadpan

response. "I'm bloody well serious. Go ahead. Take hold of the yoke."

"You're out of your mind." She folded her arms, tucking her hands close to her ribs. "I won't. I don't have the first idea what to do."

"I am right here. I won't let you kill us."

"Oh, thanks," she groaned out. "What a great choice of words."

"Quit stalling and take the yoke in your hands. I'll tell you what to do." Clearly, I would be in control of the plane at all times. She wouldn't have to do much and would certainly not touch any of the instruments. Still, I could imagine it being overwhelming.

"I really hate you for this." At the same time, she reached for the yoke in front of her, closing her fingers around the grips. "Oh, man. Oh, shit."

"That's right. Get it all out." I released the yoke, spreading my fingers, and she squealed again.

"Shit, fuck," she whispered, sitting as stiff as a board, fully upright, her frame rigid. "I can't believe I'm doing this."

"Try to relax," I suggested.

"Try to shut the hell up or take the yoke back. Either way."

"Have fun with it," I urged. "Pull back a little bit on the yoke. We want to climb a few thousand feet. See it here, on the altimeter?" I pointed out the dial. "Easy does it. A little at a time."

"Okay. I can do this," she whispered, flexing her fingers and easing back on the yoke. Her strained whimper went up in pitch, her eyes darting back and forth between the altimeter and the mountains in front of us.

"You're doing it. You're doing fine," I called out. "Level it now. Keep us straight and level."

She yelped when we leveled out, then released a shaky breath. "I did it! Oh, my God, I think I'm going to pee my pants."

"Please don't." I laughed. "Unless you feel like replacing the seat. Now, we want to turn to the left. Ease into it. We will bank, so take your time and don't freak yourself out."

Perhaps it should've come as a surprise that she took so well to flying. There was much more to learn, but already she grew comfortable with the yoke, guiding the plane without any more squealing or cursing me. Instead, she smiled and laughed as if in disbelief. It reminded me of her joy after her first ride on my Harley. We shared a love of the sort of excitement many so-called ordinary people were afraid of. She was entirely different than what I'd imagined, leaving me caught between uncertainty at my beliefs being challenged and admiration of her courage.

However, a love of excitement went only so far. When I offered to take over, her head bobbed enthusiastically. "Yes, please. Jesus, that was..."

"Better than sex?" I suggested.

For once, she didn't bother pulling a sanctimonious act. Her laughter filled the cockpit before she shrugged. "Now that you mention it, yes."

I brought the plane around, the airstrip up ahead. "If that's the case..." I quietly observed, "... you haven't had the right partner."

"No comment." A glance her way from the corner of my eye revealed her flushed cheeks. I had the feeling it wasn't entirely the effect of controlling a plane for the first time.

"I would be happy to bring you out again sometime," I sincerely offered. "You'll be a pilot in no time. Next flight, I'll guide you through a barrel roll."

"I had no idea you were so desperate to watch me throw

up," she pointed out in a shaky voice that made me laugh as I brought the plane down.

We taxied along the runway, coming to a stop. She sat completely still, staring straight ahead for a long time after the noise faded to silence. The only sound in the cockpit was that of our breathing before she whispered, "That was amazing."

"I knew you would love it." I went about unbuckling myself, more than a little regretful. We would return to the cabin now, and she would pretend none of this ever happened. The fact that I cared was a problem, but there was no denying the twinge in my chest as reality rushed back in.

She hadn't moved yet. "What's wrong?" I asked teasingly, reaching over and running my fingers beneath one of the straps across her chest. "Not ready to go back yet? Is your head still in the clouds?"

"Very funny." Her voice sounded choked, strained by the time I toyed with the buckle in her lap. Was it the aftereffect of flying or the position of my hand so close to her pussy? I felt the effect, too, my dick beginning to thicken as all manner of filthy ideas swirled in my head.

"Let me help you," I offered, noting the way she tensed when I leaned closer.

"I can do it myself," she whispered.

"Why take care of yourself when I'm offering my services?" I pressed the button to release the buckle, then pulled the straps away from her when she made no move to do so, as if she were in a trance, watching my every move before lifting her gaze to meet mine.

Something in the way she looked at me, something in those clear, sapphire depths, stole every conscious thought from my mind, replacing it with pure, blind want. Plan or no plan, I had waited long enough.

When she launched herself at me, kneeling on her seat and taking me by the lapels of my coat, it was clear she felt the same.

I thought I knew euphoria. The sense of the inevitable finally coming to pass overwhelmed me when our mouths met, when those pouty lips pressed against mine with the sort of urgency that went straight to my dick, stiffening it almost painfully before I had the chance to sink my hands into her thick and soft hair, I indulged in it as I parted her lips with my tongue.

That wasn't enough. Weeks of watching her, imagining the body beneath her clothes and how it would respond to my touch, left me greedy. Stroking her tongue with mine, I opened her coat with one hand, testing the fullness of her tits while she moaned helplessly. Firm and heavy, they set off a wave of pure longing that only grew the longer I caressed them. When she covered my hand with hers, I thought she would surely pull it away. Instead, she squeezed, silently urging me on. With a growl, I slipped beneath her sweater, fingers dancing over her lacy bra, stroking the heaving swells threatening to spill out with every ragged breath she took.

She pulled her mouth away to gulp in some air, moaning again when my lips grazed her jaw, making a path down her throat. Somehow, desperation helped her ease her body over mine in the close quarters of the cockpit until she was snug in my lap and rocking her hips, grinding her pussy against my covered erection.

I had unleashed a beast, one with the power to unlock everything I worked hard to keep hidden from the so-called civilized world. Raking my fingers across her ass cheeks, I pulled her closer, demanding more, while our tongues danced and her breathless moans filled the air. It wasn't long before I joined her, lost in the taste of her, the smell of her skin, and the sound of her needy groans. I was about to bust through my zipper, but I wouldn't have pushed her away even to ease the discomfort. I couldn't bring myself to ruin it when she was so hot and demanding, her fingers twisting in my curls, nails scraping across my scalp until my nerves sizzled.

"Oh, fuck," she whimpered close to my ear when I lifted my hips enough to grind against her. When that wasn't enough, I wedged a hand between us, pressing against her hot, plump mound, teasing the seam I felt so easily through her leggings. "Oh, my God!" she gasped out, throwing her head back and rocking faster.

Until she went stiff, sucking in a pained breath. I stopped nipping her throat long enough to find her covering the top of her head with one hand. "Fuck!" She groaned, rubbing the spot where she had hit the ceiling above us. "Shit, that was stupid."

"Are you bleeding?" I moved her hand aside, adjusting her head so I could see the top clearly. "No, it doesn't look like it."

The moment was over. I had to believe that was for the best, even if my dick did not share the sentiment. The persistent ache and the blue balls I knew would follow left me wishing we could pick up where we stopped. There was no recapturing the sort of rush that made a person throw caution into the wind.

"I guess we had better go back," she announced without looking at me. It was almost painfully awkward now as she climbed off my lap and opened the door on her side. I touched my head to the back of the seat and sighed as the discomfort of my swollen dick reminded me of what happened when I let myself get caught up in a moment.

I had planned every step so carefully, laying the groundwork always with my goal in mind.

If only I could have planned for her. How much of a struggle it would be to resist her when every part of me demanded I take her and make her mine.

She was waiting for me at the SUV's passenger side door by the time I climbed out of the cockpit, torn between regret that our moment had ended and intense self-loathing.

Because I would have given anything to take her in my arms again.

9

ARIA

Was there a world record for hiding in bed? If so, I was determined to break it on Saturday morning. Normally, I would have been up with the sun, determined to enjoy every last minute of the trip. It was another gorgeous day, with sunshine reflecting off the snow and filling my room with light. I wanted to be out there.

Some things were more important. Like avoiding Miles. What the hell had I been thinking? One minute, he had landed the plane, and I was fighting to get a handle on the adrenaline still coursing through my veins. The next?

I didn't want to think about what happened next. Throwing the blanket over my head didn't help me hide from the memory of how I had humped him like some deranged, horny teenager. The word *embarrassed* didn't begin to describe the way my soul withered every time I recalled the taste of his lips and the deep, throaty groans that had turned my pussy into a throbbing, wet mess.

And for him.

For him!

Not only my stepbrother but someone I didn't trust. I had lost sight of that somewhere along the way. It had to be the adrenaline rush. The danger. I was out of my mind with it by the time we landed. All I knew was I wanted to do that again.

And then I basically lost my mind and decided it would be a good idea to disgrace myself.

By the sounds of it, most of the house was awake. There was noise coming from the kitchen—pots and pans, the clanking of silverware. The girls would have breakfast ready soon, and I would only look suspicious if I didn't join everybody when it came time to eat. I was hungry as hell, too, and could've used an entire pot of coffee after spending most of the night tossing and turning, berating myself, regretting how easy it was to forget what I knew to be true.

I could not trust Miles. He had never bothered taking back those shitty comments he first made at the penthouse. I couldn't believe he didn't mean them any more than I believed he hadn't meant to look at me with so much contempt all those times I had noticed him watching me.

I read once that women tended to ignore their instincts and talk themselves out of following their gut. We liked to make excuses for people's bad behavior and, in some cases, would end up regretting it.

I refused to be one of those people.

That didn't mean it would be easy to look him in the eye now that he knew what my boobs felt like and how little it took to turn me into a mindless idiot searching for an orgasm.

Christ, how embarrassing.

I had done it to myself when I knew better. There was no escaping him either, here or back home. Could I not have controlled my raging hormones for a little while longer? It would've been smarter to come back here and take care of myself. Alone. In bed. I wouldn't have to dread showing my face downstairs.

"Hey! You better get down here and eat before it's all gone!" I would've known my sister's strident voice anywhere. Knowing she would only come in and physically drag me from the room, I got up, pulled on a robe, ran a brush through my hair, and eased open the door.

What had been a dull roar became a much louder one. That was one thing about the cabin. There wasn't much to dampen sound waves with so many hard surfaces and so much space.

Creeping up to the railing, I looked down to find everybody gathering. The air smelled of coffee and bacon. What a shame I was too busy hating myself to look forward to eating.

"There you are!" Valentina wore a worried, motherly look when she spotted me. "Get your ass down here or risk Lucian eating everything."

"It's only my second helping," he retorted around a mouthful of food.

Something was missing. No. Somebody. I didn't want to come straight out and ask where Miles was for fear of making it look obvious how much I cared. "Tell me you at least left some coffee," I warned on my way down the stairs.

There was no sign of him anywhere.

"I just made a second pot, but the espresso maker is on too." Rose nodded toward the machines as she sat with a loaded plate.

"Thanks." There were still two mugs sitting on the counter, one of which I assumed was supposed to be mine. I called out, "Who decided today would be a good day to quit caffeine?"

"Oh, that was supposed to be for Miles," Sienna explained, sitting at the breakfast bar and munching a piece of bacon. "But he texted Noah saying he had to go back to the city. Something about looking at an apartment at the last minute. He said he might stay down there to catch up on some work."

"Getting his offices set up," Noah finished explaining.

That should've been a relief. I didn't have to spend the rest of the weekend avoiding him, reliving every stupid mistake I made last night every time I looked at him. I could have the weekend I'd been looking forward to all this time without complications.

What a joke. The complication was already there in the form of memories vivid enough to make my pussy moisten even now as I plated my breakfast.

One thing was for sure. Once I returned to town, I had to talk to him as soon as I could get him alone. I sure as hell couldn't go on like this forever.

∽

"What do you think?"

I looked away from the window, pulling myself back from the daydream I was drowning in as Mom swept into the room wearing a dark blue gown with a full skirt and intricate beadwork across the bodice. For somebody against asking Ari for help finding something for the gala, she sure seemed to be enjoying herself now.

I loved seeing her looking so confident that she strode across her bedroom, admiring her approach in the full-length mirror. "You look incredible," I told her. "I think that might be the one."

She tapped her chin with one finger, turning to look at

herself from all angles. "I don't know. There are others to choose from. I don't want to pick the first one without trying the rest."

"Good point." I tried to inject a little enthusiasm into my voice, but I had a feeling it wasn't enough.

Turning away from the mirror, she focused on me. "What's wrong? You seem off."

Dammit. The last thing I needed was for anyone suspecting a problem and connecting it to Miles. And wasn't that funny, considering how prior to Friday night, I would have gladly admitted I was concerned about him? Then I had to go and make out with him in a fucking Cessna, making it a bad idea for anybody to pay close attention to the way we interacted unless I felt like getting my ass chewed by my parents. They were big on the whole stepbrother angle. Technically, it wasn't wrong, but there were still implications I didn't feel like getting into.

"Long weekend, lots of skiing. I tired myself out."

"It's just a shame Miles had to leave early," she mused, crossing the room so I could unzip her. "Your sister told me. It was nice of the guys to invite him. Make him a part of things."

"Yeah, they are real gems," I muttered with more than a little irritation. Things were exponentially more complicated now than they would've been if he had never shown up.

She retreated to her dressing room, and I turned my attention back to the skyline outside. *Where was he?* I hadn't seen him since we parted ways at the cabin on Friday night, with me practically fleeing to my room before I could do anything stupid like asking him to join me.

What was it about him that got me so mixed up? He had a grip on me whether I liked it or not. Ever since we'd set eyes on each other at Skye Worthington's class, he had taken up space in my brain. Space that was getting larger all the time and crowding out all of the logical thoughts I needed to focus on.

Kissing him, being kissed until every ounce of resistance melted. God, I loved every second of it, knowing it shouldn't happen and being powerless against it. For the first time in maybe my life, I had let myself get carried away and look where it had gotten me.

"What about this?" Mom appeared again in a dark red strapless dress with a dramatic train attached to the lower back. "I can take the train off if it's too awkward, but I sort of like it." The hem swished across the floor like a whisper as she approached the mirror and checked herself out.

My jaw dropped. "I know I said the first one was great, but this is drop-dead gorgeous. Honestly, I wouldn't even waste your time trying on anything else." I hoped to look half as good as she did by the time I reached sixty-five. She worked hard at it, though, that much I knew. She exercised religiously, ate well, the whole nine yards.

"How do you feel? That's the most important part." I went to her, admiring her up close while she posed and made faces in the mirror.

"I feel... really good," she admitted with a soft laugh. "Sometimes it still amazes me."

"What does?"

"You wouldn't understand because I made it a point to remind you and your sister of how gorgeous and spectacular you are every day of your lives." She caught my chin on the tips of her fingers and pursed her lips in an air kiss. "That isn't the same for everyone. I spent three decades convinced I was ugly and useless. There are still moments, all these years later, when I expect to see that girl in the mirror."

This was one of the reasons Mom had started her nonprofit in the first place. To help women who'd grown up the way she had and needed to believe there was something better they were capable and deserving of. Kissing her cheek, I whispered, "I love you. I'm proud of you. And you should definitely choose this one."

"Right. I will." She clapped with excitement, and I did the same, helping her with the zipper. By the looks of it, she would only need minimal tailoring over the next two weeks.

I couldn't believe it was already so close. I would need to take time to try on a few dresses myself. My attention was all over the place nowadays, making it difficult to stay on top of things.

"And you're still okay to help with the event on Wednesday?" Mom confirmed. I had almost forgotten about the little carnival they were holding at one of the women's centers run by the nonprofit. Hell, I had helped plan it, but the date had crept up on me while I was too distracted by Miles to notice.

Assuring her I'd be there bright and early, I retreated from the room, planning to finish unpacking the bags I had left in my room after returning earlier. That was until the sound of footsteps coming from the foyer drew me to the top of the stairs. I caught a brief glimpse of a pair of black boots and a black leather jacket before Miles disappeared from sight, having just returned from a motorcycle ride from the looks of it.

Knowing he was here, under our roof, got my nerves jangling and my heart racing. This couldn't continue. I needed him to know we could never mess around like that again. Dad would lose it, for one thing. He liked Miles so much and wanted us to be one big family. I hated the idea of disappointing him, not to mention Mom. Meanwhile,

Valentina would never let me live it down after all the bitching I had done about him.

More than anything, I wanted to respect myself again. He was my stepbrother. On top of that, I had basically told him from the beginning that I would never trust or accept him. I'd gone against all of that and betrayed myself in the process. I needed to prove I was in control of this situation. I had to. How could I look at myself in the mirror otherwise?

I was trotting down the stairs before I knew it and speed walking down the hall so I didn't lose my nerve. Light shone from beneath the door leading into his suite while the sound of footsteps reached me by the time I knocked. I regretted it immediately, but it was too late to turn back now. He was already headed for the door, his footsteps getting louder until he swung it open.

For some reason, he didn't look surprised to find me standing in before him. He only stepped aside and ushered me inside with a sweep of his arm.

And even though I couldn't shake the feeling of walking into the lion's den, I accepted the challenge and entered.

10

MILES

I knew it.

There was no chance of her staying away once she got home from the trip.

"Why did you run off on Saturday?" Aria glanced around what had to be familiar quarters. She may not have lived in this suite, but she undoubtedly had been through it countless times. Otherwise, what was the point of having so much space if it sat empty?

"Didn't anyone tell you? I had a last-minute showing of an apartment on the Upper East Side." Not true, but how could she prove me wrong? My real reason for leaving when I did was far more complex and beyond explanation. I hardly understood it myself.

"But you didn't come back." She crossed the bedroom, arms folded, her body wrapped in a bulky sweater. I liked her this way. One of those messy buns on top of her head, a pair of thick socks, and yoga pants to complete her ensemble. She was softer. Vulnerable.

"I'm opening my office within the next few weeks," I reminded her, observing her every move while I leaned against the long dresser. The king-size bed between us may as well have been a mile wide with the distance she was putting between us.

Which was a good thing. I had come breathtakingly close to destroying everything I'd worked so hard to put together by sleeping with her at the cabin and possibly being discovered. This group was hardly discreet. It might have meant losing Magnus's trust far sooner than intended. After parting ways, I had spent hours fighting the desire to kick her bedroom door in and pin her to the mattress with my body.

By the time the sky began to lighten with the first hint of dawn's approach, there had been no choice but to leave. As it turned out, it had been the right move across the board. I'd given her a reason to think of me the rest of her trip. Now, she was here, wanting answers. I was in her head. How could I not be after the heat that exploded between us in the cockpit?

"We need to talk about what happened." With her back to me, she stared out the window. If only I could have seen her face, but then her voice revealed her nerves clearly enough. "That should never have happened. We both know that."

"Since when do you put words in my mouth?"

She ventured a glance over her shoulder, her mouth screwed up in a smirk of disbelief. "You can't tell me you don't see what I'm saying."

"I see what you think you're saying."

With a heavy sigh, she whirled around, throwing her hands into the air. "Quit playing games. That's not what I'm here for."

"What *are* you here for?" Pushing away from the dresser, I began to round the bed, one slow step after another. "You don't want to kiss me again? Fair enough. Don't kiss me again. Why did there need to be an entire meeting about it?"

Her dark lashes fluttered over her eyes, swirled with confusion. "I wanted you to know in case you had the wrong idea."

"What would the wrong idea be?"

Clasping her hands on top of her bun, she shook her head. "Stop. Stop with the word games. Stop with the mind fucking. I'm sick of it."

Was there something deeply wrong with me, enjoying the sight and sound of her unraveling? "It was a simple question," I reminded her in a voice more measured than hers. "What would the wrong idea be?"

"Goddammit. I should've known better." With a growl, she started marching toward the door, and she might've gotten past me had I not caught hold of her elbow and pulled her in.

"Do you always run away when things get complicated?" Fuck, her light, vanilla-tinged perfume did something to me, along with the heat from her quickening breath fanning across my face. She tugged her arm, but I tightened my grip.

"Let go of me," she growled out. Sheer, white-hot outrage flowed through every word, tightened her muscles, and narrowed her flashing eyes.

"Stop running."

Drawing herself up to her full height still left her more than a head shorter than me. Was I supposed to be intimidated? "I wasn't running. I was removing myself from a situation where I'm wasting my fucking time."

"You're right. There are much better things we could be doing with our time, don't you think?" Confusion flickered across her face in the instant before I lunged forward to taste her lips. She gasped, shuddering like an electric current ran through her. Then took me by the back of the head and held me in place, kissing me furiously.

I hadn't counted on this. There was heat, yes, but it was more than the sort generated by two bodies in close quarters. This was more than the desire that had bloomed between us in the cockpit.

She hated me, and that hatred poured from her with every swipe of her tongue against mine, every tug of her fingers in my hair, and every sharp, short breath as I backed her against the bed, where she began almost tearing at my clothes in a frenzy, tossing my jacket to the floor and pulling my sweater over my head. Her fingertips danced over the lion's head inked across my chest, eyes meeting mine before she lowered her head to run her tongue over the firm muscles.

I'd envisioned this moment so many times in the weeks since I first set eyes on her and decided she would suit my purposes. I'd always imagined keeping a measure of control, maintaining composure, and not allowing myself to be swept up.

I may as well have decided to stand stock-still in the center of a swirling cyclone. There was no hope of maintaining a grip on myself in the force of what exploded between us once all of the anger and bitterness in me surged to the surface, met by everything she'd bottled up over the past few weeks. It was a potent combination like TNT and a lit match.

I took her by the hips and pulled her close against my raging erection, grinding against her, sinking my fingers into her flesh until she whimpered and melted against me. Her teeth sank into my bottom lip, pulling it until I hissed, dancing on the thin line between pain and pleasure.

Thank fuck they lived in a sprawling penthouse where

there was no chance that her whimpers would be heard. Because I intended to make it my mission to extract every last moan out of her. Those sounds belonged to me, and by the time I was done with her, she wouldn't be able to deny it, no matter how hard she fought me.

Working my hands under her sweater, I wasted no time pulling it over her head. My greedy hands traveled her body, measuring her firmness, the softness of her skin, those glorious tits encased in another lacy bra. A simple flick of the clasps and it fell away, stealing my breath and turning my already rock-hard dick to steel. I lifted them in my hands, worshiping them, sucking and teasing until her fingers danced through my hair, and she moaned, low and deep, the sound unleashing a primal force I barely kept a hold on when there wasn't a gorgeous woman writhing against me.

"Fuck, yes," she grunted out, her nails running over my shoulders and down my back.

I was lost in sensation.

Lost in lust...

... lost in *her*.

There was no stopping now, not when her hand brushed my aching bulge. I wouldn't be refused this time.

"I hate you," she furiously whispered while fumbling with my belt. "I fucking hate you."

No, she hated what I compelled her to do. How helpless she was when it came to me. She hated being unable to resist after deciding to dislike me weeks ago.

"That's right." My teeth scraped the delicate skin of her throat until she whimpered in my ear. "Hate me. Give me all your hate."

She offered no resistance as I pushed her onto the bed, where she flopped on her back. The sight of her bouncing tits was hypnotic, but it was the animal lust blazing in her eyes that left me hurrying through, removing my boots, and dropping my jeans. She followed suit, tearing off her leggings, leaving her in nothing but a barely existent thong. Her body was so smooth, almost glistening, and it was all mine for now.

I crawled on top of her, my heart racing in anticipation. There was no dragging this out. No teasing or building up her passion. She was already there, and by the time my fingers brushed her crotch, there was wetness causing the lace to cling to her pussy. "So wet for me," I groaned out, shuddering as our mouths met again, and she kissed me with all of the fierce, undeniable hatred her soul contained.

"Fuck me," she whispered, biting my lip, her body alive underneath mine, her hips rolling in circles to meet my caress.

I pushed the lace aside to slide a finger through her wet seam, and she arched, gasping as she hooked a leg around my ass and pulled me in. Demanding. The impatient little brat.

The only problem was I was in no position to deny her. If this went on much longer, I would embarrass myself by coming in my shorts because I couldn't have conceived of anything this hot, so hot it could burn me to ash.

"Let me get—" I forced myself to push up on my palms, planning to find a condom, but the impatient witch pulled me down again, wrapping her body around me.

"I'm on the pill. Just do it. *Now.*" She tugged impatiently at my waistband, tugging the shorts down and over my ass, scraping my skin and sinking her nails deep. Sensation flared hot and intense, ripples of sheer pleasure destroying my ability to think past the present moment. The need to take her, to fuck every last ounce of that defiance and sass out of her.

Her lean thighs spread when I stripped her thong away. Looking down between us, I took in the sight of her gorgeous, glistening pussy, her clit peeking out temptingly from between her plump lips. I longed to taste it, but for now, all that mattered was sinking deep. Losing myself in her, if only for now.

"Give me your cock," she grunted out, wrapping her fingers around my thick shaft and guiding me to where she was hot, wet, and so ready. I had built her up to this. What I didn't realize until now was how she'd built me up too.

You should slow down. You need to get control.

I pushed forward before those warnings could take hold, breaching her tight entrance and filling her in one sure, deep stroke. Her eyes closed, her head snapping back. A deep breath was followed by a long, guttural moan that left me sizzling from head to toe. There was nothing sexier than the sight of a woman coming undone around me.

I clenched my jaw against the sudden, almost overwhelming urge to give in to the temptation of release. This was new, going without a condom, with nothing between her hot, slick cunt and my cock. Like going from standard to high definition, every sensation was clearer and more intense, enough to make me shake from the effort of adjusting to it all. Once the urge passed, I pushed up onto my knees, taking her by the ankles and spreading her legs wide. She wanted to be fucked? I'd fuck her like no one ever had.

Her eyes flew open when I began taking her in hard, deep strokes, punishing her. "Oh, shit," she moaned out, her expression hardening with determination. Her hips jerked, meeting my every stroke.

There was nothing like the power of moving inside her tight cunt. Working her body, using her, allowing her to use me. I propped her legs against my chest, taking her hips in my hands and quickening my stroke until sweat coated the back of my neck and her high-pitched cries got louder.

"You like this cock?" I panted, driving her into the mattress while she writhed and moaned, her hands sliding over her tits and toying with her pink nipples. The sight damn near undid me.

"Yes! I'm... I'm gonna..." Her mouth fell open, her face contorting in pleasure. "Oh, God!"

"Give it to me," I growled out, unleashing a flurry of strokes. She used her thighs against my chest as leverage, pushing back, fucking me as hard as I fucked her. I was close, so close, the tingle at the base of my spine followed by the lifting of my balls. There wouldn't be any holding back much longer.

"I... Miles!" She stiffened, holding her breath in that final moment as she shattered around me. I took a moment to drink in the sight and sound of her orgasm, then finally allowed my own release.

The rush was incredible, overwhelming. By the time my seed dripped between us, I was spent, falling face-first beside her and wondering if I'd just finished fucking or brawling. A little bit of both, I decided while waiting for my heartbeat to slow and my breathing to ease.

I always knew I would enjoy it when things finally got physical between us.

I hadn't been prepared for the chemistry we shared, her fierce passion, or the way she fit around me like a glove.

The bed shifted when she did, and I lifted my head to find her sitting up, stretching, and sighing before throwing her legs over the side of the mattress without a word. "I never pegged you for the love-'em-and-leave-'em type," I murmured.

She stood, treating me to a view of her exquisite body. "I'm on my way to the shower." Her voice was soft and seductive as she started across the room. "I thought I'd freshen up, then we can begin round two."

My heart jumped. "Presumptuous, sweetheart?" I asked, staring at her bare ass.

Stopping in the bathroom doorway, she flipped on the light inside, then turned toward me. "Abso-fuckin-lutely. And no one can ever know about this."

"I won't tell a soul," I purred lowly, getting out of bed to pursue her into the shower. Now that that fantasy had become a reality, I didn't want to miss an opportunity to enjoy the fringe benefits of my plan.

11

ARIA

By Wednesday afternoon, spring had definitely sprung in the city. Normally, that was enough on its own to lift spirits. Pair warm temperatures with face painters and magicians, live music and jugglers, not to mention free prizes and more junk food than was probably wise to offer, and you had the recipe for some happy people at the carnival sponsored by the foundation.

"Congratulations!" I handed over a teddy bear roughly the same size as the little boy who'd won it and had the pleasure of watching his eyes go perfectly round like he couldn't believe his luck. He was overjoyed and all over a teddy bear.

"Don't forget. Not everybody grew up the way you have." Something Mom had drilled into our heads from a young age, remembering how hard life had been for her and Uncle Barrett in their youth. There was a lot neither of them would go into specifics over, but Valentina and I had spent plenty of late nights trying to piece things together after family events, especially the one Christmas when Uncle Barrett had made comments about 'that abusive fuck' when

talking about how their father treated Mom when compared to how Barrett treated Sienna.

I hated to think of my beautiful, sweet mother being abused, but it seemed possible she had been, along with her mother.

Something good had come from that. I wondered if I would have the same strength Mom did, turning my pain into purpose.

"Step right up!" I called out, beckoning passing women and children. "Try your luck!" All of the games were free. This wasn't a fundraiser. It was a way for everybody to have a good time on a sunny day.

"Hot dog?" Valentina approached with one in each hand, holding one out to me. "Brown mustard and sauerkraut, as you like it."

"Finally. I'm starving." When she smirked, I explained, "You try being happy and peppy for two hours straight and see how tiring it is. All you have to do is plop sauerkraut on hot dogs."

"You were the one who wanted to run a game booth." Her phone chimed, and she checked it, frowning. "Honestly. What's the point of having an out-of-office message in my email if somebody's just going to text me to get my attention anyway?"

"Things will calm down in a couple of days," I reminded her, referring to the club opening Friday night. As I spoke, I noticed the little boy with the giant teddy bear walking a little awkwardly as he tried to keep hold of his stuffed friend. Though it was slow going, he looked absolutely blissful.

I would ask myself the last time I was that happy, but I knew the answer. And I wished I knew what to do about it. It seemed right and wrong didn't matter when it came to

Miles. Knowing we shouldn't have slept together while wondering when we could do it again.

In all of my twenty-eight years, I had never found anything or anyone capable of shutting off my brain and turning me into a mindless animal. I hadn't known it was possible until Miles. Maybe for other people, but not for me.

The worst part? Every ounce of hatred, resentment, and mistrust had melted away like it was never there. I didn't know what to think about that or what it said about me.

"No one can ever know about this." Could I believe he would keep it a secret? When had I suddenly decided he was trustworthy? Oh, right, when my pussy started making decisions for me. Ridiculous, probably very stupid, but it was the truth. The responsible, levelheaded twin had gone off her rocker and was sleeping with her incredibly hot stepbrother. Nobody would believe it if they ever knew, which they never would. I would make sure of that.

"Oh! Look who it is." Valentina jerked her chin toward something behind me. I turned to look and damn near choked on a bite of hot dog at the sight of familiar dirty blond hair now smoothed carefully into place. The last time I was with Miles, I had tousled those curls for hours.

Where had he come from? How did he know about this? Mom had probably told him. From the looks of it, he'd come from something business-related. His button-down dress shirt and silk tie made him stand out from the crowd, but then he would have no matter what he wore, at least to me.

I watched Miles gazing across the lot, his lips stirring in something close to a smile, when three excited little girls ran past, their faces freshly painted with cat whiskers and tiger stripes. It took so little to make kids happy. It was a shame grown-ups lost that somewhere along the way—the ability to be thrilled over the littlest things like face paint or a teddy bear. When had we all become so serious?

Once Miles was looking in our direction, Valentina waved an arm overhead. "Come, try your luck!" she called out while my pulse picked up speed. He chuckled, walking our way, barely avoiding getting run over by a guy on a unicycle.

The sun was already shining, but somehow, everything felt brighter now that he was here. What was happening to me? He had a great dick and stamina to match. Was that enough to wipe out everything that had gone down before Sunday night?

I had to remind myself not to smile too wide. It was only now that I realized how much I'd wished he was there. In a matter of weeks, I had gone from hating the fact that he existed to wishing he was with me.

"How's your fastball?" I asked once he'd reached us, holding up a baseball and tossing it into the air. "Three balls for five dollars."

"Don't listen to her," Valentina warned, laughing. "It's free, and don't let her tell you otherwise."

"He can afford it." This time, I tossed him the baseball, which he caught deftly. "Do you think you can hit the target?"

He narrowed his eyes at the ball, then at the painted target behind me. A bell would chime if he hit the bull's-eye.

"I always do," he replied with a wink, hinting at a double meaning that left me fighting back a knowing grin. Valentina was right beside him, so I couldn't afford to blush. A little girl with red pigtails crept up close to where he stood, her gaze bouncing from the stuffed animals to the baseball he held. He noticed my grin and looked down at her. "If you were me, which prize would you choose?" he asked, his voice heavy and serious.

Her head tipped to the side before she flashed a gap-toothed smile. "You talk funny." She giggled.

"Not where I come from," he pointed out, solemn. "Come on. Help me choose, love."

"The pink giraffe." She didn't have to think about it. She pointed straight to the toy in question.

"That is a very wise decision." He nodded sagely, turning the ball in his hand and pulling his arm back. "For the giraffe."

There was never a doubt in my mind I would hear that bell chime. When it did, the little girl bounced up and down, clapping wildly, her gap-toothed smile almost heartbreakingly cute.

"One pink giraffe, coming up." I presented it to Miles with great flourish, leaving him to present it to the little girl who looked like her dreams were coming true as she wrapped her arms around the stuffed pink creature.

"Really?" she whispered, eyes shining, while Miles nodded.

"Look how happy you made her," I murmured as she skipped happily away to join her mother, who exclaimed in surprise at her daughter's new best friend. "That was really sweet."

"I already have a pink giraffe," he told me, winking at Valentina, who laughed before returning to the hot dog stand.

Now, it was just the two of us. At least as much as it could be when surrounded by a hundred strangers. The hair on the back of my neck stood straight, and my lace panties decided to go warm and moist without so much as him brushing against me. "I never would've expected you to come out," I admitted.

"I had time between meetings. Boring HR and administrative bullshit," he replied, rolling his eyes. "I needed the diversion. A palate cleanser."

"So everything's going well, setting up your command post out here or whatever you want to call it?" Because we had to talk about something, right? Like two normal people. Mom was no more than twenty feet away, posing for photos with some of the women and their kids. We had to keep things PG at most for the sake of young ears.

Something made his lips twitch as though he thought the whole situation was funny, watching me scramble for something to say that wouldn't give away the fact I knew the feeling of him inside me. Not with Mom nearby. "Things are going smoothly," he murmured like the prick he could be, refusing to meet me halfway as if he got off on making me squirm.

This was ridiculous. Here we were, standing around, talking as if we didn't know what the other looked like naked. He had seen my O-face, and I had watched the lion's head on his chest ripple while he pounded me as if his life depended on it. Yet we might as well have been work colleagues during a forced group activity.

"You've made yourself scarce around the penthouse these past two days," I observed quietly while rearranging the prizes that hadn't been given away yet. "Everything all right?"

"I've been very busy." His eyes shifted to the left, then the right, before adding in a lower voice, "I would love to spend more time at home, if you know what I mean, but I can't forget why I came out here. I have a job to do."

"Yes, and new offices to set up like the big hotshot you

are." I was used to it since Dad's work had been a huge part of his life for as long as I could remember. Even now, when he should've taken it easy, I passed his study throughout the day and heard tense muttering on the other side of the door. Not that he would ever share what he was up to.

Smirking, he countered, "A man does enjoy a little stress relief at the end of a long day. I wondered if we might come up with a solution for that." His hungry gaze crawled over me, leaving no question of what he had in mind. Damn my weakness for him. No matter how many times I swore to myself nothing would happen again, all it took was one look at him to unravel my willpower.

Thank God I was wearing a ball cap since it shaded my face and hid my flushed cheeks. "I think we might be able to work that out, Mr. Young," I agreed, nodding slowly while ignoring the promise I'd made to myself. "Could you pencil me in for later on this evening?"

"I'll check my schedule," he replied with a smirk. It was entirely too easy to forget myself and stare openly at him. He was very easy to look at and admire, especially when he allowed himself to loosen up and enjoy life a little.

A handful of kids ran over, excited to try their luck, and Miles stepped aside to give them space. They weren't exactly expert pitchers, but I had a box full of smaller stuffed animals under the table that stood between us. The kids who missed the bull's-eye by a mile received one of those. It didn't seem right to send a kid away empty-handed.

Miles was still hanging around by the time the kids moved on. "I don't think there are any future major league pictures in that group," I observed once they were gone, chuckling and looking Miles's way.

He wasn't smiling—just the opposite. I followed the direction of his hard, cold gaze and found a young, blonde woman scolding a boy who couldn't have been more than five or six years old. There was an ice cream cone on the ground, some of which had splashed onto his scuffed sneakers.

"I told you to be careful! Am I talking to myself? Dammit!" She swiped angrily at the shoes, not that it did much good. The chocolate ice cream was already starting to set.

The poor kid was on the verge of tears, probably more because of his lost ice cream than anything else. Valentina swooped in with a fresh cone, making it apparent she had noticed too. One of the other volunteers offered wet wipes to help clean him up a little.

The mother shook her head at my sister, scowling. "I told him he would only get one, and if he dropped it, it was on him." She then dragged the crying boy away by the arm, chastising him as she passed my booth. "Can't take you anywhere," she whispered fiercely.

I was heartsick for the poor kid, and by the looks of it, so was Valentina. Her face fell before she offered the ice cream to another little boy, then cast a dirty look at the retreating woman's back, returning to her stand.

"You all right?" I asked Miles, who continued following the woman and her son's progress as they left the lot behind the center.

"Sure. Fine." Though he was anything but. He sounded like somebody fighting hard to keep himself in check. I could only imagine that woman got to him as she had me. If this was how she treated that poor kid in public, how much worse was it at home?

"I guess it can't be easy for her," I mused, rearranging the prizes. "All of these women are single moms. Some of them are working two, three jobs to make ends meet. She's probably tired and burned out."

He was eerily silent, so much so that I checked over my shoulder to make sure he was still there. He was, and I went cold inside when I caught a flash of what I had seen in him before. The part of him I had tried to forget that I'd convinced myself was all a figment of my imagination. Otherwise, how could I have lived with myself, sleeping with him after I had practically sworn I would take him down for daring to elbow his way into my family?

"Miles?" I almost dreaded his reaction but couldn't leave him standing there, glaring angrily. He wasn't exactly giving off the right vibe for the event.

His head snapped around, and I fell back a step when the full force of his unexplained anger landed on me. "I have to go," he growled out, his teeth clenched, and by the time I caught my breath enough to ask why he was leaving, it was too late. He was already gone, weaving his way through the crowd.

Something had set him off.

And dammit, I wished he would've told me what it was. Not that I thought I could help. I only wanted to understand him.

12

MILES

"The face is looking good." The last of Josh's bruises had faded by the time we met on Wednesday afternoon, weeks after the staged fight at the bar. Staged from my standpoint, at least. I doubted it felt that way to him.

"Uh... thanks." He was still salty, but there were more important things to discuss than his personal feelings. We sat facing each other in a cramped booth situated at the rear corner of a true greasy-spoon diner in the middle of Brooklyn. The idea was to keep our activities between us, at least when it came to this particular facet of my work here in New York.

Stirring cream into a cup of bitter coffee, I asked, "Do you have it? The clock is ticking. The event is next weekend."

"I've been through everything with a fine tooth comb, and it looks legit to me." Withdrawing a manila folder from his laptop bag, he slid it across the table before picking up a greasy burger and taking a massive bite. I was glad for the excuse to avert my gaze from his sloppy feast, choosing instead to open the folder and review what was inside.

To the untrained eye, it was nothing more than a series of printouts from social media chats. Most of it centered around Facebook, though there were a few snippets of conversation taken from text messages as well, all of them going back years.

"Look good?" He wiped his fingers on a napkin, not that it did much good.

"What about the recordings?" I asked, prompting him to withdraw an older model phone from his bag. Mom hadn't upgraded it in years, though I'd offered countless times to buy her something new once I could easily afford it.

"Listen for yourself." Pulling up one of the files, he handed me the device. "Just hit play."

I did as he instructed, holding the phone to my ear in time to hear Magnus's voice. "Fuck, I miss you, Leila," he growled out. "I swear, I'm flying out there as soon as I can get away for a few days. Evelyn doesn't have a clue. You know how it is. She'll believe anything I tell her. Just know every time I jerk off, I'm thinking of you. Imagining that mouth around my dick. I can't wait until I don't have to imagine anymore, baby."

I was barely able to hold back my laughter until the recording finished. "It's perfect."

"You're sure?"

"I've spent weeks living in the man's penthouse, sharing meals, chatting about his interest in AI." Another laugh burst out of me at the irony. "Here he is, captured for posterity in all these messages."

Only he had never spoken those words, or at least not to my mother. Not within the last three decades, as far as I knew. Yet the files created using AI to mimic his voice were dated as recently as the past year, thanks to a little technical know-how when it came to doctoring data. How convenient was it that I happened to know people with such skills?

Staying at the penthouse served more than the purpose of getting close to Aria. It left me able to record conversations into which I had drawn Magnus. Most of the time, we discussed nothing in particular. That wasn't the point. Capturing his voice on my phone was all that mattered. I had, and we'd trained our new AI program using that data.

The result? Extremely incriminating recordings detailing an affair between Magnus and my mother. Along with that were the manufactured screenshots—sexting, for the most part, to confirm what the fake messages already alleged.

Evelyn would never forget the night of her nonprofit's thirtieth-anniversary gala. What a shame it wouldn't be for the reason she expected.

"You know, if he ever figures this out..." Josh winced, polishing off what was left of his burger.

"How could he? His head is so far up his ass he believes the entire world smells like his colon. Besides..." I added. "He can't prove a thing. I didn't spend so much time putting this together to leave anything to chance. As far as Magnus Miller is concerned, I'm part of his happy family. Yes, I'm about to drop a bomb on them, but there's nothing in any of this to point toward it being doctored. I am merely a concerned son wanting to clear the air." As I spoke, I scanned the printouts, carefully checking the date stamps to ensure there was nothing obvious that might give us away.

It wasn't enough to break the heart of Magnus's precious daughter. Magnus was going to regret the mistake he'd made in abandoning us and pretending we had never existed, forcing Mom to flee the country in shame—no friends or family out there, starting from scratch with her son, a paltry excuse for a divorce settlement, and no support system.

My chest tightened when memories from earlier in the afternoon slammed into me. That boy, his mother. She could have been Mom. How many times had she berated me mercilessly for a stupid accident? How many times had she made it sound like she blamed me more for my very existence than for a glass of spilled milk or a grass-stained sweater?

It wasn't her fault. She had done the best with what life had given her. The drugs and the drinking had already begun to change her by the time I was roughly that boy's age, perhaps a year or two older. Until then, she had only been short-tempered and unpredictable, but there had been some good times. Fun times.

"You okay?" Josh asked nervously, eyeing me warily from across the table. "Something wrong?"

"Nothing you need to worry about." I snatched the folder and the phone, then dropped bills on the table to cover his meal and my coffee. "My thanks to your people for this."

"My people? I only found them because you told me to," he reminded me. The man was uncomfortable, to say the least, nervous at the idea of facing Magnus's wrath.

"I have no idea who they are or where they do their work, which means they're more your people than mine." By design, naturally. The less I could be associated with this, the better. "We'll touch base tomorrow on progress with the office renovations."

"We could do that now," he pointed out, speaking to the back of my head. I was already on my way to the door. There was no need to blur the line between work and vengeance.

When all was said and done, I would look like nothing more than an innocent bystander who wanted to set the record straight for Evelyn's sake. By then, Aria would at least be half in love with me. She was already in my clutches, something I couldn't pretend I didn't enjoy. They were fringe benefits. I might miss her when it was over and had no choice but to move on, leaving the ruins of a happy family behind me. It didn't matter that there was a media empire within the extended family. Connor Diamond would not be able to suppress the news once it spread. It would, too, thanks to my revealing Magnus's supposed betrayal during a gala packed with friends, family, and society figures.

I was so close. I almost tasted victory as I left the diner and took a cab into Manhattan. I didn't want any proof of this meeting, not Uber records or a ticket from a parking garage. I went out of my way to cover my tracks the way I had all along.

Soon, Mom. If I were a spiritual man, I might have believed she'd sent that woman and her son to me as a sign today, reminding me what this was about and why it mattered. How completely miserable and hopeless she had felt for so very long and how it had all trickled down onto me.

My phone buzzed halfway over the Brooklyn Bridge. A text from Aria.

Aria: *How about we relieve some stress with a movie tonight? 8:00, home theater. I'll start without you, so don't be late.*

Yes, sweet little Aria. Crave my presence. Come up with reasons for us to spend time together. The Manhattan skyline spread out before me on the other side of the bridge when I looked up from the message, and I smiled with satisfaction. One day, I would own this town.

For now, I would settle for owning Aria's body for the short time we were still together. I would make these last days count.

Me: *Careful, or I'll have to ravish you before the movie's over. You know it drives me crazy when you get all demanding.*

13

ARIA

It was five minutes to eight. A large bowl of popcorn sat between two of the deep, plush seats in our home theater. We had spent so many happy hours here, Valentina and I, sometimes with our friends, sometimes with Mom and Dad. We used to curl up under blankets, sometimes covering our faces if the scene was too scary. Horror movies had always scared the hell out of me when I was a kid, but somehow, it wasn't as bad when I knew I was right down the hall from my bedroom. I was safe.

Was I safe tonight? Debatable. Obviously, it was a waste of time to tell myself this was wrong, that we shouldn't spend time together this way. Somewhere, when I wasn't paying attention, I had stopped caring about that.

It's probably because I started caring too much about him. This would've been so much easier if there hadn't been the chance to get to know him. It was always harder to hate someone I knew.

It didn't hurt that he was an expert at making me come until my ears rang, and I forgot how to speak.

I settled in, confident he would join me, and he didn't disappoint. The door opened behind me, leaving me holding my breath, staring up at the screen where the Blu-ray menu for the movie I had chosen was displayed.

"Fuck." Was that admiration in Miles's voice as he approached, passing two rows of seats before reaching mine? "Why go out in public at all? You have everything you need right here under this roof."

He had a point. "It was something Dad put together for Valentina and me," I explained, patting the seat on the other side of the popcorn bucket. "We always had the coolest sleepovers."

"No doubt." The strange, unsettling anger that had seemed to grip him earlier at the carnival was nowhere in sight. Grinning affably, he dropped into his seat, now wearing a sweater and jeans with only socks on his feet. This might have been the most casual I had ever seen him. Well, not counting the time we were naked together.

"Oh, I forgot. Are you thirsty?" I hopped up and scooted over to the mini refrigerator in the corner. "There's Coke, root beer, Dr. Pepper."

"I'll have a Coke," he decided. "I still can't get over how nice this is. Your father spared no expense on you two."

"Mom always worried he was spoiling us," I confessed, bringing him a soda and settling down with one of my own. "She didn't grow up this way. She kept us grounded." He grunted softly but offered no reply. I probably seemed like the least grounded person who ever lived.

"Have you ever seen *Citizen Kane*?" I asked, picking up the remote. "And if not, would you mind watching it now? It's probably my favorite movie."

"I've never had the pleasure," he admitted. "Though it's

always been on my list of films I would like to check out. There has to be a reason it's so highly regarded, I imagine."

I clapped my hands gleefully before remembering whose presence I was in. "Don't laugh at me," I warned when his lips twitched as if he was about to do just that. "Sorry, I get excited when I have the chance to introduce people to something I love."

His smile was genuine. "That's very nice. I look forward to the film." He took a handful of popcorn and tossed a few pieces into his mouth, grunting in approval. "Shit, this is good."

"I aim to please." His eyes held mine as I pushed play on the remote.

Sitting next to him, every nerve on edge, I couldn't ignore his nearness and the electric touch of his fingers grazing mine as we both reached for the popcorn bucket at the exact same time. The tension between us was palpable, heightened by the soft gasps and murmurs he made in response to the twists of the plot. I was determined to keep my eyes glued to the screen, but damn, it was a struggle with that pull toward him.

Every so often, I'd glance his way. There was nothing as gratifying as watching somebody enjoy something I loved. After a while, he noticed, his gaze locking onto mine.

I didn't stand a chance against him. All it took was the sight of those gold-flecked orbs to light a fire in my core. Something wicked sizzled through me like a lightning bolt, and I slid out of my seat before there was time to talk myself out of it.

"What are you doing?" he asked, amused, as I lowered myself to my knees. I gave him a quick glance, sliding my hands under the hem of his sweater to unbutton his jeans.

Why use words when actions get the point across?

He watched my every move, completely still and almost holding his breath when I lowered his zipper. What was I doing? Anybody could come in if they heard the movie playing and wanted to join us. He had no reason to lock the door when he came in.

That didn't stop me. I didn't know what would now that a wicked little sizzle danced up my spine. Finally, what I'd always heard made sense. Danger made the whole thing much hotter.

I opened his fly and reached inside his boxer briefs to pull his stiffening dick through the opening at the front. I knew how big he was. He had damn near split me in half. Still, having him in my hand left me wondering if I could take him into my mouth.

I had to try. It was the challenge that drove me to run my tongue around his ridge, making him tense, releasing a deep breath, and sinking into the seat. "Fuck, that's good," he groaned out, barely audible over the movie playing behind me.

His hand found the back of my head as I took him into my mouth, letting him slide past my lips. I held him there for a second, taking him to the edge of his patience before plunging my head down as far as I could go. Already, the salty taste of his precum danced across my tongue.

There was a sense of power, which was why I had always enjoyed giving head. Being in control of a man's pleasure, setting the pace, slowing down if it seemed he was rushing toward the end.

Now, it was even better. There was more than a feeling of power surging through me as I bobbed rhythmically up and down, using my tongue to massage the bundle of nerves under his head with each stroke. This was Miles I was sucking. For once, I was in control, and I was going to savor every second of it.

I released him with a soft, popping sound, followed by his deep groan. "Put it in your mouth," he ordered, pushing on my head like that would help.

Stroking him with my hand, I shook my head. "You don't call the shots now," I warned, giggling when he groaned again in dismay. "Sorry."

"No, you aren't," he muttered miserably. That misery ended when I licked his head like a lollipop before plunging down again, sucking harder until there was nothing he could do but grunt with every breath, all of his control slipping away while the music reached a crescendo that filled the room as I took him to the edge.

"Yeah… just like that… you're gonna make me come…" he whispered, lifting his hips, frantic for relief. I moved faster, letting his sharp gasps guide me until he groaned, his hand tightening around the back of my head, pulling my hair an instant before he filled my mouth with a rush of salty warmth that I quickly swallowed back, keeping up, somehow needing to prove I could take all of him. A strange sense of pride swelled in my chest when he finished.

I released him and reached for my soda, taking a long gulp as I stood. The movie was over now, the sled burning up in the fire and sending plumes of smoke into the sky. "Sorry I made you miss the end of the movie," I murmured.

In the soft glow from the screen, I caught sight of his wide grin. His eyes were closed, his heaving chest slowly starting to settle down. "Are you kidding?" He sighed. "That was the best fucking film I've ever seen. It could be we need to go to your room to discuss it a bit more."

What was already warm and wet suddenly started to ache at his choice of words. "I think I could spare a little time for some film discussion," I agreed while he tucked himself into his pants.

This was bad.

It was so bad.

Then why did it feel so good?

14

MILES

"Tell me." Settling back in my chair, I crossed one ankle over the other knee. "What's it like going out for boys' night when two of you are settled down?"

Colton and Noah exchanged a glance, both of them smirking. "Different," Noah announced. "Not in a bad way. But different."

"I sure as hell don't mind." Evan snickered, lifting his glass to the two of them. "More for those of us who choose not to get tied up with one pussy for too long."

"Watch it," Colton growled out. It was amazing how he could suddenly go from affable to murderous. "Don't talk about my girlfriend that way."

"Or my sister," Noah added, narrowing his eyes, but it didn't last long before he chuckled, jerking a thumb at Colton. "Or his sister, for that matter."

"You mean to tell me the two of you didn't kick each other's asses over that?" I found it difficult to believe either of them would have been all right with the other fucking their sister. It was sort of a code, even I knew that, but I'd never had close friendships like theirs. Acquaintances at most. Roommates, classmates. Nothing like this. Nothing with history.

"Noah tried," Colton told me with a smirk.

Holding up a hand, Noah insisted, "I held myself back for Rose's sake. I didn't want her to watch me beat the shit out of you."

"A likely story," I concluded, and laughter rose among the five of us.

"Oh, Miles." Colton lifted a hand to signal for a server. "Did anyone talk to you about my parents' anniversary party next week? Tuesday night. It was the only time the old folks could agree on."

"I hadn't heard anything about it," I admitted. "Would it be appropriate for me to be there?"

He nodded, almost laughing off what seemed to me a reasonable question. "I'm sure they would love to meet you." I could believe that, strangely enough. Even Magnus and Evelyn struck me as genuinely warm and welcoming after weeks spent under their roof—time had clearly softened them. What a shame it did nothing to change the shitty choices they made in their younger days or the consequences of those choices.

Lucian caught my attention when he placed his empty glass on the table, rolling his eyes as he did. "What he means is... our mothers can't wait to get a look at you."

"Here comes something I would like to get a look at." Evan wore a charming grin that all but melted the panties off our server, who took a few moments to eye fuck him before looking around the rest of the group.

I could understand what they meant about having more women to go around now that two of their members were spoken for. The girl attempted to get Noah's attention, yet he only offered a brief, friendly grin then checked his phone. What would that be like, meeting the single woman with the power to make all other women disappear? I'd never imagined it possible. The sort of fairy tale people enjoyed telling themselves—true love and all that bullshit.

I followed Noah's lead, looking at my phone and ignoring a handful of emails from associates. Even I couldn't bring myself to care about HR issues and staffing questions at half past ten on a Friday night. There were limits. Boundaries.

"Where are the girls tonight?" Evan asked.

"Oh, they stopped off at that new club in the meatpacking district. The one Valentina was promoting." Colton checked the time. "They'll be out for a while still."

I hadn't crossed paths with Aria this evening. Why was that so strange? Something felt off. Unfinished. Spending the past two nights together, we'd made a private joke of the term *film discussion*, always using that as our excuse to escape to one bedroom or the other. It already had me craving her beyond all reason. Soon, there would be no choice but to forget her, but an entire week stretched between then and now.

A smart man would have set his sights on another woman—any woman. They surrounded us, orbiting our table like satellites, hoping to be pulled in by one of us, and doubtful it mattered which. I had my pick of every height, weight, hair color, and skin color. A veritable smorgasbord awaited me.

Yet I felt empty. Flat. Uninspired. Rather than take advantage of a willing stranger, I pulled up our text thread and shot Aria a message.

Me: *What are you wearing?*

Risky? Perhaps. There was always a chance someone

might see. Pretend all she might, we both knew she got off on a bit of excitement. The thrill of knowing she was a bad girl. Something told me she hadn't gotten much experience being bad before we met. How fortunate I was to open her up and broaden her horizons.

She didn't keep me waiting. While fresh drinks were served, her text came through.

Aria: *Clothes. The same as I always do.*

"What's so interesting?" Evan noticed my grin and craned his neck, attempting to peer at my phone.

"Your mom was reminding me of how good she is at tonguing my balls," I retorted, shoving him away with a laugh. "Obviously."

Noah coughed hard enough to raise a few worried looks from passersby. "Oh, fuck," he choked out, laughing again. "Warn a guy next time."

"That was good," Colton agreed. To his credit, Evan laughed it off. There was something almost unnerving about that. How willing they were to accept me as part of their group. There had been no trial period or point where I was expected to prove myself worthy of their esteem. They had simply given it to me. Granted, my flashy toys may have helped a bit, but they could only take a person so far.

Returning to my phone, I tapped out another message. Now that I'd caught her attention, there was no resisting the urge to play a little.

Me: *How about sending me a pic? For visual aid purposes.*

She must have been as keen to screw around as I was since she replied almost instantly.

Aria: *How about waiting until I see you later?*
Me: *Since when have I been that patient?*
Aria: *I'm convinced you're the devil. You know that, right?*

It took biting my tongue to suppress a laugh. She only

thought she knew. Rather than reply, I laid the phone face down on my lap, certain she wouldn't disappoint.

"I'll see you guys later," Evan spoke, staring across the crowded bar. Clearly, he'd found his diversion for the evening. I caught a glimpse of a leggy blonde staring at him before my phone buzzed with a new text.

"Fuck," I breathed out, nearly dropping the phone once I'd opened the photo she sent. My eyes darted left, then right, then I dared steal another glance of Aria's shaved pussy. Either she'd gone out without underwear, or she'd taken them down for me. The result was the same, regardless. A potentially painful erection began to stir.

Tucking my phone away rather than risk exposing her more than she'd exposed herself, I cleared my throat. "What do you think about checking out that new club?" I suggested. No way was I waiting to see her at the penthouse after she'd thrown down the gauntlet. Her little stunt deserved to be matched.

Noah shrugged, looking around. "I wouldn't mind catching up with Sienna."

"More like whoever is trying to hit on her," Evan predicted with a smirk as he approached his muse for the evening.

Looking my way, Noah grunted. "You're the one who fights in bars. Kick his ass for me, would you?" Yet my suggestion had done the trick, the others standing and checking their pockets as Colton settled the tab.

On the way across town, I sent Aria another text, my heart beating faster now that it was a matter of minutes until reality would replace a photo.

Me: *Go to the ladies' room and wait for me. Be there in five.*

She would have a dozen questions, none of which I would answer until we were face-to-face. By then, there wouldn't be a need for words to teach her what happened to girls who sent me nudes to tease me—even if I'd started things.

"Valentina outdid herself," Colton observed as our car pulled up in front of the club.

We cut our way through the crowd with ease—camera flashes going off around us, voices ringing out as a long line of partiers waited to get past the velvet rope holding them back. I didn't see exactly how much cash Noah tucked into the palms of each bouncer, but it was enough to get us inside with no problem while a handful of would-be guests grumbled behind us. The music was damn near deafening, and I recognized a handful of famous faces as we entered the club's main room beyond the front desk.

"How are we supposed to find them in all of this?" Colton shouted and scanned the room of roughly a few hundred people, where most of them danced, posed for photos, and drank plenty of what was probably overpriced alcohol.

"I need to find the restroom," I called out. "If I run into anyone, I'll let them know we're here." It made sense to head deeper into the club, assuming the bathrooms were in the rear. There was a short line of women waiting by an open door. Was this the only restroom? I would have to take a chance. Surely, I couldn't be the only man in existence who'd ever sneaked his way past a line of impatient women.

"Hey! Where do you think you're going?" the girl at the front of the line demanded, hands on her hips, while a chorus of female voices rang out behind her.

"I need to pick up my girl," I called out. "She texted she was sick in here."

"We'll get her for you!" another woman further back in the line insisted, but I pretended I didn't hear her, nudging my way through the open door and passing a pair of giggling women on their way out. They eyed me and giggled harder but made no attempt to stop my progress.

Half a dozen stalls were in there and a row of sinks across from them, topped by a mirror running the length of the wall. Women clustered there, checking their makeup and complimenting each other. "Aria?" I called out, catching everyone's attention. "My girl is feeling under the weather," I explained with an apologetic smile.

"At the end of the row!" she replied. I headed straight in that direction, biting back a grin, and eased the metal door open to find Aria waiting, arms folded, scowling.

"How are you feeling, love?" I managed to wait until the door was closed before chucking at her irritation. She wasn't irritated enough to deny my demand, was she?

"I met you in here," she whispered fiercely, tapping the toe of a strappy stiletto heel. "Okay? I took the dare."

Right. Because that was all I'd had in mind. Even if it had been, the sight of her in a tight leather skirt and low-cut, sleeveless top would have changed my plans. She had pulled out all the stops tonight, and the thought of other men ogling her luscious body left me glad I'd joined her before any of them made the fatal mistake of putting a hand on her.

"What are you doing?" she whispered as I slid the latch side to lock the door.

My answer was covering her mouth with mine, tasting vodka and olive brine lingering on her lips. The dirty girl liked dirty martinis. "You think you can tease me like that, and I won't have to attack you?" I whispered, kissing her again, my tongue halfway down her throat by the time my hands slid beneath her tight skirt. Turning, I backed her against the door and pinned her there with my body.

The hands she pressed to my chest tightened to fists, clutching my shirt once the simple act of igniting her passion was complete. I raised the skirt to her hips, and she lifted a leg, wrapping it around mine, grinding her hips in a frantic attempt at humping me. While voices overlapped and echoed on the other side of the metal door, she slid a hand between us and lowered my zipper.

Just when I thought I had the upper hand, she insisted on topping me. "Bad, bad girl," I whispered in her ear, breaking the kiss, my tongue teasing her lobe. She arched against me, and I fisted my cock, guiding it against her seam, my dick jumping at the contact with her wet folds. She was still pantiless, the naughty thing.

"Where's your panties?" I hissed before stroking the head of my cock between those plump lips. She pressed her face to my neck to muffle her high-pitched cry on contact with her hot flesh.

"My purse," she breathed out, bearing down on me, rocking her hips against my hand then taking my rigid cock in hers. Pure lust made my head spin before I claimed her mouth again to muffle her whimpers as I slid two fingers deep inside her tight cunt. She was bad for me, only for me. There was something surprisingly hot about it, knowing I was turning her into a risk-taker.

"Who's in here?" a woman called out from the other side of the door while Aria stroked me, using precum to lube my shaft. Her fist moved in a blur, and I matched her speed, pounding my knuckles against her sensitive flesh. The end was just ahead, rushing up on both of us.

Suddenly, she went stiff, her mouth hanging open in a silent scream as her muscles contracted around my fingers. I reached out blindly for the toilet roll and pulled a handful free to catch what shot from my tip a moment later. By the time the rush passed, I was weak in the knees and laughing softly at what we'd done.

Aria slapped my shoulder, then held a finger to her lips. "Let's not be too obvious," she whispered, squeezing her eyes shut. "I can't believe that happened."

She was still sandwiched between the door and me, and I couldn't resist taking advantage of that, kissing her until she sighed, melting the way she always did when it came to me.

We had so little time left together. I had to take every opportunity to enjoy her before no chances were left. Fuck, I was going to miss this.

"You know what I think?" I asked, brushing my lips against the tip of her nose. "You're an adrenaline junkie."

Snorting, she shook her head, then went through the motions of straightening out her clothes and hair with trembling hands. "I'm the furthest thing from it."

She didn't have me fooled. I caught her pleased smile when she thought I wasn't looking.

15

ARIA

"Happy anniversary!" I threw my arms around my Aunt Lourde before doing the same to my Uncle Barrett when I entered their penthouse apartment. They had been out of the country for a month to celebrate their anniversary and had deep tans thanks to all of the sun they'd gotten sailing around the Mediterranean.

"So this is Miles." Aunt Lourde extended both hands toward him when he entered behind me, followed by Valentina and our parents. "The things you miss when you're traveling. I'm Lourde Black. Colton and Sienna have already told us so much about you!"

"And you're still welcoming him into your home?" I teased, winking at him.

"Don't listen to Aria," Valentina announced, kissing our aunt's cheek and hugging Uncle Barrett. "You two look amazing."

"Are we the last ones to arrive?" Dad asked when Mom greeted her brother. They shared the same strong, special bond I shared with Valentina. It was nice to see them still getting along so well for so long.

"Everyone else is back in the living room," Aunt Lourde informed us, draping an arm around Mom's waist and leading her from the entry hall into the spacious living room with windows overlooked Central Park.

As promised, everyone was there. Ari and Olivia sat close together on the sofa, his arm around her shoulders. Connor and Pepper sat opposite them with her feet tucked underneath her, obviously having kicked off her shoes at some point. They chatted warmly like the old friends they were while Colton mixed drinks at the bar in the far corner by the windows. Whatever story Lucian was telling had him and Noah in stitches while Sienna and Rose rolled their eyes at each other. Boy talk.

"Hey, Miles!" Colton lifted a hand when he spotted Miles. "Are you a scotch man? Dad brought back a bottle of Macallan 1937. He bought it from a collector. You'll love it."

"I've been known to sample scotch from time to time," Miles replied, and I had to give it to him. Somehow, he had managed to fit himself seamlessly into our group. I'd resented him for it at first. Now, I admired him since I had never been somebody who found it easy to fit in right away. When I was a kid, there were times that I'd wondered if I would have any friends if it weren't for the close-knit group I had grown up with.

I could admit to myself as I sipped a glass of ice-cold Chablis courtesy of Sienna that I had resented Miles for that more than I'd wanted to admit to myself. It was so easy for him to be accepted by everybody—Mom, Dad, my sister, and all our friends. Had I been using that deep-seated jealousy as another reason to mistrust him? Probably. As if it was his fault he was so easy to like.

"This is exquisite," he announced, smacking his lips and

studying the bottle Colton had poured from. "And rare, by the looks of it."

"I couldn't pass up the opportunity," Uncle Barrett called out as he helped Aunt Lourde carry two large charcuterie trays into the living room. It was like nobody present had ever eaten before, everyone descending on the elaborate array of meats, cheeses, and fruits. It meant all of us gathering together around the central coffee table, perched in chairs, cross-legged on the floor, telling stories like we had so many times throughout my life.

Most of the stories revolved around either my aunt and uncle's anniversary trip or their wedding. Considering it had been thirty years since they were married, it surprised me how clear the memories were, how easily they tripped off the tongues of the older adults.

"I have one word for you, ladies." Aunt Lourde was giggling as she snagged a piece of sharp cheddar, pausing before popping into her mouth. "Headbands."

Mom hooted with laughter, covering her face with her hands. "How could I have forgotten about those?"

Pepper shrugged, offering a smile when Olivia and Lourde turned her way. "Hey, I got a good deal on them. And let's not act like everybody didn't have a blast wearing them."

"I seem to remember all of us dancing our asses off on that boat, wearing those silly things," Olivia reminded everyone.

Valentina and I exchanged a confused look. "What headbands?" she asked.

Mom's face went tomato red while Dad chuckled. "The headbands your mother and the other ladies wore the night of Lourde's bachelorette party featured very large, glowing rubber penises on top."

Rose shrieked with laughter while Sienna's mouth fell open. "How did I not know about this?" she asked.

"They bobbed around when we moved," Mom continued, wiping tears of laughter from her eyes. "I completely forgot."

Dad pulled her in for a hug, the two of them seated next to Connor and Pepper. "And then I found you with that stupid headband falling over your eyes. Imagine that," he continued, looking around the room, chuckling. "She was blinded by a flashing purple dick."

"Oh, my God," I muttered, rolling my eyes. "Very classy, Dad."

"It was a bachelorette party," Pepper reminded us. "That's kind of the point. Classy has nothing to do with it."

"It didn't seem to turn you off any," Mom pointed out, smiling fondly at Dad. At times like this, I could imagine them when they were young. They may as well have been those two young people thirty years ago, falling in love. "It didn't stop you from giving me our first kiss that night, did it?"

"I must've been hard up. Newly single and all that." Dad laughed when she nudged him like she was indignant.

"Please, tell me we're not going to get more graphic," Valentina warned as she stood, holding up her glass on the way back to the bar. "We don't need tonight turning into an episode from a wildlife documentary."

Laughing, I looked toward Miles, sitting in one of the leather easy chairs at the far end of the coffee table. He wasn't laughing. Instead, he was staring at my parents, his brow pinched together like he was either in pain or deep in thought. I waited for him to look my way and lifted an eyebrow when he did, silently wondering what the problem

Sinful Desires 151

was. He only looked down at his glass, his lips drawn into a thin line.

What was that all about?

I forced myself to focus on other things rather than staring at him in a way somebody was bound to notice. "I could use some more wine, too," I announced, getting up from the floor and grabbing my glass. "Anybody else?"

On my way past, I touched Miles's shoulder. "Would you like a refill?"

"Perhaps a sip more," he allowed, standing. "As long as Barrett is feeling generous."

"Go right ahead," Barrett urged with a wave of his hand. "Enjoy it."

We retreated to the corner, where I stepped behind the bar and reached into the refrigerator for the bottle of wine. Miles poured himself more of the fine scotch, turning away from me and staring out the window. Something had gotten to him. I was almost overwhelmed by the desire to know what could have upset him so much.

"Are you okay?" I murmured, glancing around the room as I did. Nobody seemed to notice the way he brooded, swirling scotch in his glass, making the ice cube clink against the sides.

When I touched his shoulder, he snapped out of it, his forehead creased in confusion when he looked at me. "This is their thirtieth anniversary," he said.

"That's right. I mean, they were out of the country on their trip, so we're celebrating it now. But it's pretty close." Why did he look so confused? It wasn't like they didn't have anniversaries over in England.

"And your parents..." He looked at them over my shoulder, and I did the same. Dad had his arm around Mom's waist, and she was smiling, her forehead touching his shoulder while he chuckled over something. I had seen them that way so many times. The casual intimacy, the ease they had with each other.

"The first kiss was thirty years ago?" he muttered. "After the divorce?"

"Yeah. Is there something wrong with that?" I blurted out a disbelieving laugh. "They got together the weekend of the wedding. I mean, they first noticed each other that way. It's sort of a nice story, right?"

"Sure." He took a gulp from his glass, releasing a shuddering breath after swallowing.

It wasn't the first time a fleeting thought had passed through my mind. What if he felt weird, wondering what life would have been like if he were Dad's biological son? If Dad and Leila had stayed together. By the time my parents first got involved, Leila was already the past. Mom was the future. Their lives took two completely different paths.

The sudden dimming of the lights tore my attention from him. We both turned in time to see Colton and Sienna wheeling a cake in from the kitchen, candles glowing on top. "Happy anniversary to you…" Sienna began, and we all picked up the song as we gathered closer to the happy couple.

Except for Miles. He joined me, but he didn't join in the singing. It seemed like he was looking through the cake, through all of us, somewhere else completely.

And it was unnerving how desperately I wanted to bring him back to me.

16

MILES

She was asleep, her light purple locks spread across the white pillowcase. I had never seen someone sleep as deeply as Aria. A bomb could have gone off, and it wouldn't have disturbed her. Just for the hell of it, I moved around a bit, enough to jostle her. It didn't so much affect the rhythm of her breathing.

She was on her stomach, one arm bent across the pillow, the sheets twisted around her naked body in an enticing way. Covering all the important bits but hinting at a variable playground of delights I'd already sampled after returning from the anniversary party. Valentina had headed to her apartment while Magnus and Evelyn had hung back to relive their glory days a little longer.

What a shame I couldn't have joined her in sleep. There was something burning in me, a red-hot coal lodged in my chest. Two rounds of almost exhausting sex hadn't been enough to douse it. Nothing would.

The timeline didn't make sense.

No matter how I went over it in my mind, I couldn't make it line up. Mom had always been adamant about

Evelyn stealing Magnus from her. Yet Magnus had referred to himself as newly single when reminiscing about their first kiss. Meaning, I assumed the divorce was in process or had already been finalized.

Someone had to be wrong somewhere. I didn't want it to be me.

No, I couldn't be. Fuck, Mom had driven the tale into my head more times than I cared to count. Some children were brought up reciting prayers at bedtime or reading fairy tales. I grew up with an ugly story of betrayal burned into my young consciousness.

"He couldn't even dump me in private to leave me with a little dignity." Mom's vicious recounting was vivid, chillingly so. *"He had to wait until his asshole friends were throwing an engagement party to stand on a chair and tell me to fuck myself in front of half of Manhattan that he was in love with Evelyn. I became a joke. Nobody took my side. I couldn't show my face in public after that. I used every last penny I had to fly to England for a fresh start, along with my baby boy,"* she would always conclude, and somehow her already vicious tone would become harder and colder. *"I wish I had stayed behind. I could've looked that bastard in the eye when he refused to pay more than a pittance in the divorce settlement. I'm sure he tipped his housekeeper more than he gave me after destroying my reputation and making me a laughingstock in front of all those people."*

I rolled onto my back, the silk sheets cool beneath my overheated body. I was too hot inside, burning with indecision. Should I ask Magnus for his side of the story? It didn't matter, and it wouldn't change anything. Besides, it might tip him off if I appeared too interested in the past. He might realize I didn't buy his version of history.

Was he as two-faced as I was always led to believe? I

couldn't make the image Mom drilled into my head match up with the loving family man I'd observed at the party earlier—adoring husband, doting father. Had time worked its charm on him?

Doubt had planted itself and was beginning to grow. All because of a story about a first kiss. It left me grinding my teeth against the impulse to bang down Magnus's bedroom door and demand answers.

Who was I kidding? He wouldn't tell the truth, only his version of it. Mom was no longer here to defend herself. He was bound to say anything so long as he came out looking like the hero, the way he always tried to do. Mr. Generous, an all-around good guy who had disgraced his wife in front of everyone she knew and mocked her with his new relationship. I couldn't trust him. It would be foolish to let a few weeks of generosity undo decades of pain and struggle.

"You're still awake?"

The last thing I'd expected was to hear Aria's soft, sleepy voice beside me. "You aren't asleep?" I countered in surprise.

"Not right now." She yawned, somehow managing to make it look adorable, rubbing a fist over her eyes. "What's wrong?"

"Nothing. Go back to sleep." I sat up, reaching for the foot of the bed and the duvet bunched up there. I shook it out, then spread it over her. "It seems I have a lot on my mind."

"You know, you can talk to me about it." She rolled onto her side, yawning but determined to stay awake. "I could tell you were deep in thought earlier at the party. You don't have to hold everything inside."

If only it were that simple—a matter of getting over my male pride and the stoicism that seemed to be bred in many of us. "Things have been busy with work. Nothing you need to worry about. I shouldn't let it get to me while I'm in the company of others."

"You're only human," she murmured. "It's okay. And sometimes, my family can be a little overwhelming. Everybody has this long history and a million inside jokes. They all talk over each other, they bust balls. It's a lot to take in."

"It had nothing to do with that." I wished it had. I could handle ballbusting. "I envy you that. Your family. That history. No one..."

What the fuck was I doing? I hadn't intended to go down this winding, twisting path. She didn't need to know, and I doubt she wanted to know about me. No one ever had.

"Go on," she whispered. Her hand touched my chest, resting before she began tracing the outline of the lion's head. "What made you get this?"

If anything, I was glad for the sudden change in subject. "It's a symbol of strength. The king of the beasts."

"That's how you see yourself?" There was soft laughter in her voice and something else. Sexy, flirtatious. It stirred something in me and left me wanting to pull her close. For her to cling to me so I could hold her closer. What the hell was happening in my head? A simple party and I was untethered, uncertain of myself.

"That's what I am," I replied with a grin I didn't feel.

"So what were you going to say before you cut yourself off?" She propped herself up on her elbow, her hair spilling over my shoulder while she gazed down at me. I had accused her of running away once. Now, that was all I wanted to do. To hide from her. It would have been too easy to confess everything. And that was all I longed to do.

All my life, I'd never had anyone to confide in. None of the close friendships Aria had known. The friendships her parents knew. I'd been isolated, if not consciously on my part, then as the result, being different from everyone else. Poor, hungry, and sometimes in dirty clothes until I was old enough to collect spare change from our apartment to pay for the laundromat.

I wanted to tell her. The words were there on the tip of my tongue, ready to spill over my lips. So many years. So much shame. Nobody understood that kind of shame. Not her, that I was certain. Being ashamed of something there was no control over. It wasn't my fault Mom's life turned out the way it had or that we had no money. There'd been no way for me to control any of it. Yet I had grown up feeling the need to apologize for being who I was or how I was—friendless, poor, no siblings, and a mother absent most of the time. She barely made ends meet even with all the work and the hours she'd spent away from me.

"It must've been nice for you," I mused, stroking a strand of her hair and staring at it to avoid having to look at her and be seen. "Having all these people who cared about you. Knowing there was... a net. Something to catch you if you fell."

"You didn't have that?"

I shook my head. "Nowhere near it. You were right about it being overwhelming, but not for the reason you thought. They seem like good people." For the most part. They weren't what I'd expected, that was for certain. Aside from Magnus and Evelyn, I have lately found myself wishing I could be part of them—sitting back, having drinks, bullshitting about work and life, and creating memories together like we had in Vermont.

I would never be part of this because there was no scenario where this ends happily. It couldn't. I had come too far.

She pressed her lips to my shoulder, lingering there for a

long time before she kissed my cheek. "Why don't we go to sleep now?" she whispered in my ear, running a hand through my hair.

"Right. We should." I draped an arm around her, pulling her close. Her head rested on my shoulder, the sweet scent of her hair lingering in the air as I closed my eyes and reminded myself where all this had started. I'd come too far to turn back now. There were other women for me to turn to once this was over. I would build a life as soon as I'd avenged my mother's.

If only I could make the timeline work. I went over it again, staring at the ceiling long after Aria fell asleep.

She could afford to sleep well. She would never understand what it meant to lie awake at night and question what she'd once believed was a fundamental truth.

But if I were wrong, that would mean my mother lied to me, fed me poison all my life, and turned me against the very people I was raised to despise. My whole world would be a lie.

17

ARIA

He was pulling away.

By Friday night, I could feel it after spending an entire day without a single word from him. Not that he'd sent more than a couple of texts on Thursday complaining about being busy. I was losing him, watching him slip through my fingers with no explanation.

Ridiculous. He never belonged to you. It didn't matter how many times I'd told myself that in the last few days leading up to the gala. Granted, Mom kept me busy working with the event coordinator, double checking a few late RSVPs, confirming allergy requirements with the catering staff at the Saint Regis. It wasn't as if I had a ton of time to spend with Miles or that I should have been spending time with him, anyway.

There was a reason it mattered so much that I kept us a secret. I didn't want Dad threatening to chop Miles's balls off for touching me. That didn't mean it hurt any less when my texts went ignored, like the one I'd sent at lunchtime.

Me: *Hanging around the penthouse today. Waiting for dresses to be dropped off. Will I see you?*

I hadn't seen him since Wednesday morning when I woke up in his bed around dawn. He had already been up and getting dressed for a workout. Two days later, I shivered at the memory of how cold it felt in that room. Something had literally changed overnight. He was so unsettled after the party at Uncle Barrett's. I still couldn't put my finger on what might have gotten to him. No amount of scrutinizing every word of the conversations at the party brought me any closer to figuring him out.

It was silly to read too much into him—his thoughts, motivations, and past. The way he grew up was so unlike the way I had. I was overanalyzing it, wasn't I? I couldn't help it. I had never met anyone so determined to be an enigma. I had never so much wanted to solve a mystery as I wanted to solve him.

By the time dinner rolled around without a word from him, I was damn near beside myself. It was as if I was an addict needing a fix. How had I existed before him? I could barely remember. How was that possible?

The penthouse was as silent as a mausoleum. Mom had gone to the spa for a night of pampering with Aunt Lourde in preparation for the gala, and Dad was having dinner with the so-called hunk holes. I couldn't count the number of times I had rolled my eyes at that nickname.

That left me alone, wondering if I should go out, not really wanting to. My heart wasn't in it.

By the time I puttered around my suite on Friday night after ordering way too much sushi and applying a facemask, I had the feeling I was in too deep. Bumming around on a Friday night, eating dinner in my bedroom while feeling sad and confused because the boy I liked wouldn't text me back —what was this, high school?

It sure as hell seemed like it since my heart almost burst

out of my chest when my phone buzzed with a text from him.

Miles: *On my way from the garage now. Long day.*

My hands trembled with excitement. Right away, I wanted to make his day better somehow. Boy, I was in trouble.

Me: *Are you hungry? I ordered an ass ton of sushi. I'll never be able to eat all of it. I'm in my room.*

Miles: *An ass ton? I might have to come up just to see how much an ass ton of sushi is.*

He wanted to see me. That alone was a relief. It helped me release the tension I'd been carrying around in me ever since things got weird on Wednesday. I tossed the phone on the bed beside the half-eaten containers of food, running for the bathroom to take off my mask and quickly brushing through my hair.

By the time he knocked on my bedroom door, I had tossed off my hoodie, leaving me in a pair of soft pants and a tank top. How was I supposed to know he would only text from the garage and give me no time to look a little less grungy?

He had taken off his suit jacket but was still in his button-down shirt and navy slacks. He looked tired as he removed his cufflinks and stepped into the room, eyeing the half-eaten feast. Along with that was my MacBook, where I'd been binging episodes of *British Bake-Off*. "So this is what girls do on Friday night that they don't want guys to know about," he mused, picking up the spare pair of chopsticks and snagging some fresh tuna.

"Oh, it gets much worse than this," I told him, sitting at the foot of the bed while he sat near the head. "There's a whole blood sacrifice thing, but that has to be performed precisely at midnight, or shit can get really dark."

"Good to know." Some of the tightness melted from his face when our eyes met, and he offered a weary smile. "Hi."

"Hi," I whispered. "You look beat."

"That makes sense since I feel rather beat." Popping a piece of salmon and mango roll into his mouth, he added, "This helps."

I had to be close to him. What was this compulsion? The absolute all-consuming desire to touch him instead of sitting and watching him eat. I climbed onto the bed and crawled up behind him, kneeling so I could take his shoulders in my hands and knead them. "You're too tense. It feels like I'm trying to massage granite."

"It's those final days, you know? Everything's coming to a head."

I giggled softly, nudging him. "You sound miserable. Aren't you looking forward to expanding your business out here?"

"I've been looking forward to this for a long time," he murmured. "That doesn't mean it's easy."

"Of course." Taking a chance, I leaned closer, letting my arms slide around his chest for a hug. "You've come really far. Don't lose sight of that now."

What did I expect? Something more than a half-hearted pat on my arm, I guess. There was something off with him, and I sensed it went beyond work. How was I supposed to help if he wouldn't let me in?

Who says he wants your help? I hated that stupid, reasonable voice in my head. The way I felt went beyond logic and reason.

He craned his neck, turning his head to offer a brief grin. "Afraid I've polished off most of this," he observed, gesturing with the chopsticks toward the now mostly empty containers.

"No worries," I assured him. "I always tell myself if I order too much, I can eat the rest tomorrow, but it's never as good the next day." He got everything together and left it on the nightstand before kicking off his shoes. Somehow, that tiny gesture warmed me from head to toe, knowing he wanted to get comfortable with me.

I cared way too much, and it scared me. But so long as I was being honest with myself, it was a good kind of fear. A roller coaster fear, a bungee jumping fear. I would be safe in the end.

Wouldn't I?

My train of thought brought with it a flash of inspiration. "I know what will relax you. Maybe we should go take a ride on your bike."

"I don't know." His disinterested response made my heart sink, but I did my best to hide it. "I'm tired."

He must have interpreted my crestfallen expression because he stood and took my face in his hands. "Otherwise, I would love to take you for a ride," he murmured, stroking my cheeks before kissing the tip of my nose. "I'm really tired and slow, and you're much too precious to take chances with."

Just like that, all was forgiven. How did he do it?

It helped when he kissed me slowly and deeply, sinking his hands into my hair and holding my head in place so he could explore my mouth with his tongue until there was nothing to do but moan my encouragement. I was already wet, hot, and shaking, working his shirt buttons, spreading it open, and treating my hands to a tour of his exquisite chest and rippling abs. He pulled the shirt from his waistband, and I slid it away from his shoulders and down his arms before letting it drop to the floor.

"Thank fuck, this house is huge so no one can hear your

moans," he teased as he began exploring my bare skin, sliding the straps of my tank top down my arms, lowering his head to pepper kisses against my shoulders and across my collarbone. He knew by now the hint of danger, perceived or real, got me hotter. I would swear my skin was sizzling with every ripple of sensation going straight to my clit. It almost hurt, it felt so good.

When he pulled the tight tank over my head, I was shaking with need, moaning when he extended his tongue and flicked it across the tip of my nipple. "Or yours. Even so, we'll have to be quiet," I decided, biting back a moan when he scraped his teeth over the sensitive flesh.

"You think so?" Something wicked flashed across his face when our eyes met. I knew I was in trouble when he yanked my pants down to my knees without warning. "Turn around on your hands and knees for me. Let me see that beautiful ass."

I was most definitely in trouble. That didn't stop me from doing as he said, getting on my hands and knees with my ass in the air. "Perfect." He growled, his hands sliding over my cheeks, making me bite back another moan. I would bite straight through my lip before much longer, but I wouldn't have stopped him for anything, especially not when he yanked down my thong and ran a finger between my already slick lips.

"And the most beautiful pussy," he continued, teasing my pussy with one hand, my ass with the other. I had to grab a pillow and press my face to it when there was no containing the mind-blowing heat building in my core and spreading through the rest of me. This was what I was missing. What I was afraid I wouldn't have again when enough hours had gone without hearing from him. I was so sure it was all over, but now here I was with Miles working me the way only he could. The way only he ever had.

The way I wanted only him to do. "More... please," I whispered, pushing back against him.

"That's right. Keep doing that." He lowered his zipper as he whispered, adding a thumb to my clit and working it in circles until I moaned into the pillow again. "Fuck yourself on my fingers, baby. Make yourself come. Let me watch."

Throwing my hair to the side, I looked over my shoulder and found him staring down at the place where he entered me. I realized he was stroking himself with his other hand, transfixed, and the thought of him jerking off to the sight of me practically tore my body to pieces thanks to the sudden, toe-curling orgasm that ripped through me.

It was still coursing through me when he climbed up behind me and replaced his fingers with his wide head, pushing forward and filling me all at once. Instead of coming down, I was suspended in complete ecstasy, shaking uncontrollably.

"Don't scream, now," he warned in a breathless whisper, taking me in deep, almost punishing strokes that rocked me forward. "Be nice and quiet while I fuck this pussy. While I come inside you. Is that what you want?"

I didn't trust myself to raise my head, so I settled for grunting and pushing back against him the way I had before. It was incredible, the way he filled me, almost stretching me beyond what I thought I could handle. And even that had pleasure in it, knowing he could take me to my limits and then beyond.

"So fucking sweet," he whispered, his breath coming faster. "Maybe I should come on your ass instead. Paint it with my cum. Would you like that?"

I would like anything just then, with my body heating

and nipples pebbling at his words. I didn't know anything but this, right now, each stroke pushing me closer to oblivion. I welcomed it, worked for it, and never doubted he would take me there.

Though he surprised me, pulling out when I was seconds away from the finish. My dismayed moan was cut off when he flipped me onto my back and settled between my thighs. "No, this is better," he decided, entering me again, this time lowering himself to his forearms and teasing me with a lingering kiss as he began to move again.

He was right. This was better. Looking up at him, watching every muscle in his face react to the pleasure, to the heat building where our bodies joined. "Come with me," I begged, sinking my teeth into his shoulder to stifle a moan.

"Can you be a good, quiet girl?" he asked, grinding his teeth and slamming into me. Determined to break me. He wouldn't.

"Yes," I whispered, then bit my lip when his body crashed into me again.

I would never want anyone the way I wanted him, and this was why.

Nobody knew me the way he did.

Nobody left me wanting and needy like he did.

Nobody challenged me.

Nobody made me want to hold them like he did.

To comfort, protect, play with, fight, and come together like this at the end of the day and remember what it was all about—this fundamental connection.

I didn't want him with my body. I wanted him with all of me.

"Come for me," he grunted out close to my ear, moving faster, breathing harder. There was no resisting. I couldn't have stopped the tidal wave if I tried. I gave myself over to it, to him, letting go before he drove himself deep one last time and groaned in my ear.

I couldn't breathe, and it wasn't because of his weight on top of me. It was because my heart was too full, expanding past my ribs, crushing my lungs, filling me with light, and making me wrap my arms around his shoulders, holding him close, running my fingers through his hair as he shivered in the aftermath.

It came out before I could help it. It was like water splashing over the top of an overfilled glass. "I think I'm falling for you," I whispered in the sweaty, breathless afterglow.

Somehow, he went even heavier, as though his body sagged against mine before he caught himself. My heart went from warm to icy in the blink of an eye, my body stiffening. It was a mistake. I never should have said it. How could I have been so stupid?

"Aria…" He raised his head, doubts and confusion swirling in his eyes as he gazed down at me. I hated to see it and know he had doubts.

"It's okay," I assured him with as much of a smile as I could manage. It was better to gloss over my mistake than to bear the discomfort of what I had just set in motion. "Don't worry about it. Forget I said anything."

I wouldn't forget. I would worry about it a hell of a lot—about my feelings and why he looked so distraught once I had shared them.

18

MILES

The work was about to pay off—the hours of research and planning. Tonight, it all came to an end. For Mom. For me.

"You look so handsome." Aria's hand brushed mine as she stood on her tiptoes, murmuring in my ear as hundreds of partygoers mingled around us. "I can't wait to tear that tux off you with my teeth later."

My treacherous body warmed at the idea before I could help it. "I'm looking forward to it," I lied, offering a brief smile as she hurried off to join Valentina and Evelyn for a photo beneath a banner proclaiming the foundation's thirty years of existence.

They made a beautiful trio, but naturally my gaze lingered on Aria in her floor-length, backless dress the same shade of blue as her eyes. I would've enjoyed tearing it off her later if there would be a later.

I needed a drink.

Local reporters milled about, conducting short interviews for puff pieces on the eleven o'clock news. Camera flashes went off at every turn while a band dressed in tuxedos and floor-length black dresses played peppy standards. Champagne flowed like water, and I took a flute from a tray as a waiter passed. It would have to do until I found the bar, but navigating the packed ballroom was damn near impossible. I hadn't imagined there being this many guests crammed in here. So much the better when it came time for Evelyn's perfect life to come crashing down.

The envelope in my breast pocket felt heavier than it should have as I carried my champagne to the table designated for the family. Evelyn had left her red clutch on her chair after our arrival, and now I dropped to one knee as if tying my shoe before opening the small bag and tucking the envelope inside. It protruded slightly, meaning she'd be more likely to notice it and investigate.

The culmination of everything I'd worked for, the fulfillment of a promise. Across the front, I'd written Evelyn's name, tucking the folded printouts and slim Android phone inside. Along with that, I'd included a short note explaining my desire to set the record straight. *I am only trying to be fair to you and my mother's memory.*

It was finished.

Now, there was nothing to do but wish I could take Aria in my arms on the dance floor. Sienna and Colton were out there, along with Ari and Olivia Goldsmith and Connor and Pepper Diamond. We could have been out there with them if only I could've forgotten what this was all about. I couldn't do that. If I'd fallen for Aria somewhere along the way, that was my weakness. Mom deserved better than that.

Draining what was left in my glass, I reminded myself what this was all about. The sight of Magnus leading his blushing wife onto the floor helped stiffen my spine. He would pay with each accusation she hurled. And with every tear Aria shed.

She had to be around somewhere, though we'd agreed it would be smart to keep our distance to avoid being found out. To her, this was still some sexy game—hiding us from her friends and family. If anything, she owed me for opening her eyes and forcing her to abandon childish illusions.

"Excuse me. Are you Miles Young?" I hardly had time to register the presence of a middle-aged woman at my side before her hand grabbed my arm. She wore too much perfume and a king's ransom in diamonds. "It must be you. You're the image of your mother. I heard you were in the country. I've been hoping to run into you somewhere."

As if I didn't have enough difficulty maintaining a pleasant expression tonight. "Forgive me," I managed, trying to keep an eye on the table across the room where Evelyn's surprise waited. "Do we know each other from London?"

She attempted a smile, though her face hardly moved. "Leila and I were friends. We modeled together for a few years."

My pulse spiked at the thought of meeting someone who had known her. She had never used names, so certain she'd been entirely written off by everyone back here. I had no point of reference, no means of tracking anyone down and demanding to know why they turned their backs on her. Every question I ever had for these nameless, faceless fucks rushed to the surface and threatened to pour out, but there was something more pressing, more immediate. This was someone who could tell me about her.

"Yes, I am Miles Young." Shaking her hand, I found it difficult to narrow my questions to one or two. "You knew my mother? I've never met any of her friends. I admit, I've often wondered about what her life was like in the States."

"Leila was a firecracker," she said, laughing. "It's such a

shame she wasn't as successful as I was when it came to finding a rich man, or she might never have left the country." She touched a bejeweled finger to her red lips. "Shh... don't tell my husband."

She was obviously tipsy, but alcohol had a way of uncovering the truth. "I'm afraid I don't understand."

"Oh, you know. *Magnus*," she mouthed, rolling her eyes. "Word gets around. He welcomed you with open arms after meeting you at the funeral. He's a lot more forgiving than he used to be, but then time heals things. Some men are willing to look the other way when their wives play so long as they have something nice on their arm on a night like this. Others don't have the patience. Thankfully, my husband does."

Subtext ran beneath her words, elusive, beyond the reach of my fingertips. "What are you trying to say?" I asked in a remarkably measured tone. "Did my mother have an affair?"

"*An* affair?" She blurted out a bawdy laugh I imagined was enhanced by the amount of champagne she'd consumed. "Like I said... firecracker. No man could tame her. She picked the wrong guy, I guess, but she got plenty out of it in the end. The idiot didn't have her sign a prenup, so she was taken care of either way." Again, she held a finger to her lips, looking back and forth like she was sharing a secret. "Considering the fact that you're here, I assume there's no bad blood."

She laughed again, placing a hand on my arm. I understood that touch. She was hoping her husband would look the other way yet again. "Come to think of it, we've met before. You were living with her mother, barely more than a baby. Of course, I swore to keep you a secret."

I could only stare in blank confusion. "Leila never told

you *anything*, did she?" she asked with a giggle. "She wouldn't have wanted to tell you about her schemes back when we were young, hot and hustling. She never did find the right time to dump you on him. She figured Magnus wouldn't want anything to do with a child who wasn't his, so she kept coming up with reasons to postpone telling him about you. After he divorced her and she had already run through a chunk of the settlement, she considered using you to appeal to him to take her back and give you a stable life. The single mother angle, you know? She wanted to give you the best of everything. I know she did."

Her nails bit into me through my shirt sleeve and jacket. "But it was too late for that. He had moved on. I only wish Leila had stuck around instead of running away, but I guess she closed and locked the door on this life when he confronted her at that party and called her out. From what I heard, she left the country not long after."

I was almost grateful for this nameless woman's claws in my arm. They may have been all that tethered me to the ground. My throat had gone dry, but I croaked, "What you're telling me is my mother was married to Magnus, and they divorced after *she* had an affair. All the while, he had no idea I existed. By the time Mom decided to use me in a last-ditch effort to get him back, he was already with Evelyn and she never got the chance."

"That's the long and short of it," she concluded with a sigh. "We all do what we have to do."

"Excuse me." I barely got the words out. I hardly heard them, the screaming in my head louder than the music, the chatter, all of it. The room spun when a sick, cold sweat coated the back of my neck.

The envelope.

The note.

Sinful Desires

Everything I thought I knew was a lie.

To hell with propriety. I damn near knocked a handful of women to the floor as I cut through them, almost running for our table. *Please, don't let her have found it. Please, please. Let it be sitting there.* It had to be there.

I launched myself at the chair and pulled it away from the table, only to find it empty. No. No, it couldn't be. I checked every chair, my head on a swivel once I found them empty. Where was Evelyn? Where was Magnus?

Where was Aria?

If I couldn't find Evelyn or Magnus, I had to get to her before they did. Had to explain what now seemed inexplicable. That woman—whoever she was—had no reason to lie. My mother, on the other hand, had lied to me all my life. She might even have talked herself into believing her lies over the years.

And Aria's heart would be crushed under the weight of it all.

I almost missed Noah and Lucian attempting to get my attention but pulled up short before barking, "Have you seen Aria? It's important."

Noah's brow creased in concern. "I just saw her leaving the ballroom as we were coming in."

Fuck. Had she been crying? There was no time to ask. I jogged toward the double doors leading out of the room, where handfuls of guests chatted and networked in the hall. A series of smaller rooms sat across from the ballroom, all of them dark and empty, with the lobby further down the hall bustled with even more guests.

I spotted a flash of sapphire blue silk and followed it, weaving through the crowd and catching Aria before she could escape to the ladies' room up ahead. She turned and smiled to find me holding her wrist, telling me she didn't know yet. A small miracle. "I need to talk to you. Immediately," I murmured, eyeing one of the empty rooms nearby. "It's an emergency."

"Oh, my God." Her face paled. "Mom? Dad? Is there—"

"They're fine." Not true. By now, nothing was fine. Without another word, I pulled her into the closest room, almost dragging her away from the open door to avoid being overheard.

"What's wrong?" she asked once we stopped. "You look like you've seen a ghost."

"I may have." What was I supposed to say? Whatever it was, I had to say it fast. The clock was ticking. "One of Mom's old friends. She told me... Aria, she told me something I didn't know. I swear, I didn't know."

Those eyes. So blue and trusting were gazing up at me. I was about to drain the light from them. No one could blame me for taking one more moment to memorize how she looked a heartbeat before everything fell to pieces.

I took her face in my hands, fighting to breathe as I drew her closer. "I made a mistake."

Darkness fell over us when someone stepped into the doorway. I turned to find a familiar figure silhouetted against the light from the hall. "That is a serious fucking understatement."

Aria jumped away from me like I was on fire. "Dad!" she gasped. "What are you—"

"Get away from her." Magnus took one menacing step after another into the room, his attention trained squarely on me. "Aria, you should go."

He knew. Of course, he knew. I was too late. "Let me explain," I urged to no avail. He merely sneered.

"You fucking snake," he grunted out. "I welcomed you into my home. Encouraged my family and friends to accept you, knowing you came from a lying, deceitful woman who was never anything but misery to anyone who cared for her. Did you think you had me fooled?"

"Dad? What is happening?" Aria asked. "I'm a grown woman. I can do what I want."

"And this?" He thrust an arm her way, glaring at me. "Hacking me, I can forgive. Digging into my past? I have nothing to hide. If you had come to me as a man, we could have cleared things up. But you chose to go behind my back."

His dark eyes were murderous by the time he concluded, "And you dragged my family into it. My daughter. I could break your neck."

I almost wished he would when Aria's choked sob cut through the icy silence. "What is he saying?" she asked me, tugging my arm. "What did you do? You hacked him?"

"It was only an attempt. He did much worse than that." Magnus pulled her away from me, and I let her go without a fight. I had no defense. "It's a good thing I warned your mother in advance not to trust him."

When my eyes widened, he barked out a brutal laugh. I had underestimated the man. I'd been wrong about so many things. "I thought spending time with us would be enough to put an end to your bullshit," he spat. "That was my mistake. Leila's blood flows through you, and you're as irredeemable as she was. Now, I want you out of here. Out of this hotel, out of our home, out of our lives. I'll have your things sent to you."

"Whatever he did, there must be an explanation." Aria's chin quivered when she looked up at him. "There has to be."

Turning to me, she begged, "Tell him. Tell him it's a mistake."

"He created audio files using AI to make it sound like I

left explicit messages for his mother." Magnus growled. "He gave your mom a phone full of them, not to mention printouts of fake text conversations with Leila to make it look like we were having an affair for years. And he left it for her tonight of all nights, out there in the ballroom. All in hopes of destroying her, me, our family."

Now her entire body shook. She leaned against her father, staring at me in horror as the truth sank in. "Say it isn't true," she pleaded in a thin whisper.

I couldn't. Nor could I tell her how much I regretted what I'd done to her. Not in front of him. He would have laid me out on my ass before I managed three words.

All I could do was lift my chin and face the aftermath of what I'd brought about—the destruction not of Magnus Miller but my own.

And Aria's.

Though I would rather have squeezed my balls in a vice than watch her crumble, I forced myself to witness her face falling before she covered it with her hands. I deserved it after what I'd done. Magnus shot one final look of complete disgust my way, wrapping her in his arms.

Taking that as my cue, I left the room and soon headed out of the hotel without another word to anyone who'd been kind enough to welcome me into their lives, knowing I'd never forgive myself for being such a fool.

And that I would be lucky if Magnus chose to leave things where they were.

19

ARIA

Until now, I'd only thought I knew what heartbreak was. I hadn't gone twenty-eight years without ever falling in love or breaking up. I hadn't had a ton of boyfriends but enough to toughen me up a little.

Or so I thought.

It wasn't losing Miles, which would have hurt plenty on its own. The pain went so much deeper than that. Loss paired with betrayal. Looking back, going over every moment, conversation, and stolen glance, I asked myself what was really going through his head. How many times he'd laughed at me, and how easy it had been to make me fall for him and his lies.

Even that, I might have been able to stand. The way I imagined I would've been able to stand being cheated on. Sure, it would've hurt like hell for a long time, but I would've gotten over it.

Knowing he wanted to hurt my family? There was malice behind what he had done. *That* I couldn't get over and doubted I ever would. Who could?

I had fallen for him when he was counting down the days until he could destroy us.

The worst part was I still didn't understand why after a week of hiding in my childhood bedroom.

What was I supposed to do? Call him? Even if I had wanted to hear his voice again, which I didn't, no matter how my weak heart told me otherwise, how could I believe a word he'd say?

Days went by without me keeping track of morning or night. I didn't bother checking the time, and I sure as hell didn't check my phone, which I had turned off completely by the end of that awful, ugly night. Somehow, Mom and Dad had managed to maintain the image. As far as I knew, everybody in our circle was now aware of what went down, but beyond that? Not a single guest had a clue. Miles's big plan to humiliate my innocent parents had fizzled out.

I'd been humiliated enough for all of us.

Sleep was the only way to escape the pain of betrayal, hating myself for letting myself be betrayed. Every so often, I would open the bedroom door a crack after getting up to use the bathroom, and there would be a tray waiting for me on the floor in the hallway. Mom and Valentina had eventually given up on trying to get me to talk. I hadn't bothered unlocking the door when they knocked. I ate the bare minimum and left the rest before crawling back into bed and wishing I could sleep until everything passed. How much time would that take? I didn't have the faintest clue.

How could he do it? How could he live with us, lie to us, and allow himself to be accepted and even embraced when he knew all along what he planned to do? What kind of sociopath did that?

Oh, right. The sociopath I had fallen in love with.

I was shattered. I didn't know where to begin putting myself back together again.

Eventually, there was a knock on the door for the first time in days. Heavy, almost pounding, telling me it wasn't Mom or my sister. "Aria. I want to see you in my study. Right now. Don't make me seek out the spare key for this door."

Dad sounded stern, maybe even angry, but I could see through him. He was worried. Considering this was the first time he had tried to reach out to me since the party, I figured it had to be important. I didn't much feel like obeying, but I wouldn't have put it past him to kick the door in if he couldn't find the key. I didn't have it in me to witness that when I was already on the verge of tears most of the time. But it meant dragging myself out of bed, grabbing a hoodie from my closet, raising it over my messy hair, and wrapping the rest around me like armor.

I wanted to disappear inside it.

I wanted to disappear, period.

The rest of the penthouse was dead silent by the time I eased the door open and crept downstairs. Dread had me feeling jumpy, wondering what he had to tell me.

He was sitting on the leather sofa across from his desk with two steaming cups of coffee in front of him and a small plate of cookies. The clock on the bookshelf told me it was barely past ten in the morning. "It's early in the day for these, but I remembered how much you like the chocolate chip cookies from Levain," he explained, gesturing toward the plate. "And you need to eat something. It's not the healthiest choice, but it's better than nothing."

They did look good, and the coffee smelled great. Still, I would've refused them if he didn't look so worried. The least I could do was meet him halfway and snag a thick cookie before sitting on the other end of the sofa, my feet tucked under me.

"You don't know how worried we've been this past week," he murmured.

"I'm sorry I worried you," I mumbled, picking at a chocolate chip.

He leaned forward to grab a cookie of his own and took a big bite, chewing slowly. "I'm sure you have questions. You deserve them answered. I have a few of my own, but it can wait." The wry note in his voice told me he was talking about my personal relationship with Miles. We were not going to touch that. I couldn't handle it.

"I don't know what to tell you, anyway," I confessed. "It happened, it shouldn't have, it's over."

"I wish I had known. You have no idea how much I wish I had known so I could've put a stop to it. You were never supposed to get hurt. I wanted to keep you and your sister out of this."

Until now, I had only thought about myself—the lies, broken trust, feeling used and stupid. Now, I sat up a little straighter, setting the cookie on the table and giving him my full attention. "How did you know what was going to happen? What do you mean, you wanted to keep me out of it? What the hell was going on all this time?"

The antique clock ticked away the seconds as I waited for answers. Dad picked up the coffee in front of him, took a big gulp, and cleared his throat. "Months ago, there was an attempted hack of our in-home network," he explained. "Naturally, I have people who keep an eye out for things like that, and it was squashed before anything could come of it. But there were more attempts, and they were traced to servers in the UK. It happened I'd recently gotten word of

Leila's passing and had planned to fly out for the funeral. I didn't first make a connection until I met Miles."

God, just the sound of his name was a sledgehammer to my chest. It left me blinking back tears and forcing myself to listen to what came next.

"No matter what he thought, I'm not some drooling old man without a clue how the world works. What I didn't know was how far he planned to go," he admitted, his voice heavy with sorrow. "I would never have invited him to stay with us if I knew the full scope of his plan included you."

I swallowed the lump in my throat, asking, "But you did know there was something sketchy about him?"

"I did. No matter what he told you, I had no idea he existed until we met at his mother's funeral. I knew right off he was too old to be mine. Besides, she would have screamed for child support the second the pregnancy test turned positive. I knew he had to be the product of a fling prior to our getting married."

"Okay..." I wanted to accept him at face value, but the brief bit of background he gave me raised red flags. Why would he pretend to trust somebody he knew had ill intentions?

When I arched an eyebrow, he explained, "Miles told me she raised him alone, never remarried, and he hinted vaguely at her being ill for several years. Since I hadn't heard anything about an illness, per se, that was when I began to do a little digging. Leila had a hard life and made it everybody else's problem," he concluded with sadness in his voice. "Unfortunately, even with all the opportunities I gave her to live more securely, there was no saving her. She clearly squandered the divorce settlement, and that was after she blatantly cheated on me during our marriage. I had no idea there was a child involved all that time. Remembering her and the way her brain worked, it only made sense that she'd fed him vicious lies about our marriage and why it ended."

He lifted a shoulder and released a weary sigh. I couldn't remember the last time I'd seen him this way. For the first time in my memory, my father looked his age. "I knew if he was dead set on hating or at least resenting me for whatever reason Leila planted in his head, coming straight out and telling him his mother was wrong would be a waste of breath. I guess... I guess I hoped spending time with him, letting him see us, the way we live and treat each other and how much we care about one another..."

"You should've said something," I whispered, shaking as anger started leaking into my awareness the longer I thought everything through. "You told Mom you didn't trust him. Why couldn't you have told me? I was living under the same roof with him all these weeks. Didn't I deserve to know?"

"Looking back, I see how much sense that makes." When all I could do was stare at him in disbelief, he closed his eyes and groaned. "I might've thought I was protecting you. I honestly can't remember anymore. I never expected things to go that far. I was determined to beat him at his own game and make him regret screwing with me. I lost sight of everything in his orbit. I only hope you can forgive me for that."

"What are you going to do now? With him?" I couldn't say his name. I could barely handle thinking about him, picturing his face in my head, not to mention other things like the sound of his voice and how his touch lit me up even back when I had wanted anything but to crave him.

His eyes opened, narrowing into slits. "I have a few ideas in mind, not the least of which being the dismantling of his company. Once word gets out in the press of his methods in applying his AI technology, not to mention the assholes he associates with him, hackers and the like, he won't have a chance. I've considered buying what's left at bargain basement prices," he concluded. "To throw it in his face how easy it was to take everything from him when he started this planning on taking everything from me."

I wouldn't lie to myself and pretend the idea didn't excite me. Watching Miles dissolve in disgrace, the way he deserved after seducing me, using me, using my family and friends, trying to break my parents up to ruin us.

There was something else, something bigger, something that turned the lingering sweetness in my mouth harsh and bitter. "You lost sight of the rest of us because all you cared about was punishing him for screwing with you. You let him think he was getting away with it so you could hold it over his head when the time came."

"That's not completely true. I just explained—"

"And you didn't trust me enough to even warn me," I concluded, unfolding my legs, standing on them even though they trembled. "None of this had to happen. I can't believe you let it go when it didn't have to happen."

"Aria." He began to stand, but I shook my head, backing away. I wasn't in the mood for a hug. I didn't want to look at him.

"I'm going to pack my bags and be out of here by noon," I announced. "The apartment will be finished soon."

"What?" he barked. "Where are you going to go?"

"A hotel. Anywhere. Just not here."

"I never imagined you getting hurt," he insisted, rounding the sofa and pursuing me out of the room. "I thought it was all about me."

"Exactly. There is your problem." I couldn't look at him

anymore. Even if I knew he had the best intentions, I was hurting too badly not to take the first opportunity to hurt the person closest to me. Just then, that was my dad.

At least he was smart enough not to follow me when I ran down the hall, blinded by tears. It was a good thing I knew the layout so well.

20

MILES

Magnus: *I want to see you in my study. 3:00 p.m. sharp.*

If anything, the text from Magnus couldn't have come at a better time. After a week of tormenting myself, cursing every decision I had made for months, regretting taking my mother's stories at face value, seeing him again would at least bring an end to things.

I deserved whatever he had in mind.

Nothing could be worse than what I'd put myself through—a week of questions, forcing myself to go back through memories to see what I'd missed. There was something to be said for beginning indoctrination from a young age. I was living proof of that. From the time I was a small child, I'd been given a version of events. As I'd gotten older, it had never occurred to me to question what I'd been told.

All of those late nights were spent alone and hungry. Mom hadn't gotten home until three or four in the morning, usually with a new man. Men who would give her money. Now that I had begun thinking, memories I'd forgotten for years came rushing back, hearing her ask one of her dates for money to buy groceries before he left in the morning. Had she bought groceries? Had she purchased new clothes for me when she came home with bags full of new items for herself? She used to call them work clothes, though looking back, I couldn't imagine the sort of job she would have dressed for in knee-high leather boots and a nearly sheer tank top. I didn't believe she was a prostitute, but she'd used men for money, certainly. Once they'd gotten tired of her antics, she had moved on to the next.

It was her doing—all of it. I'd been so damn blind, hardened beneath layer upon layer of the same stories, accusations, and excuses.

Now, I was on my way to face my fate. Magnus had made good on his word to send my things to the suite at The Plaza. Other than that and the text he sent earlier, I'd had no contact with anyone involved with him or his family. They had written me off. They had every right to do so.

It was Aria I missed most. My body craved hers until I couldn't think, eat, or sleep. The memory of her distraught expression, the pain in her eyes, and that quivering chin seized my heart and stole my breath a week later. I would have given anything to take it back and hold her one more time. Anything more than that was beyond what I deserved.

Riding the elevator to the penthouse meant the possibility of meeting with her. No, he would never ask me to meet him at home if there were a chance I would see her. If he destroyed my life, she would be the reason why. Forget what I'd done to him. I had hurt her. That was unforgivable. I knew I certainly would never forgive myself for being so fucking blind.

It wasn't Magnus who answered the door when I rang the bell. "Miles." Evelyn opened the door wider and stepped aside. "Magnus is waiting for you in his study."

Gone was the warm, welcoming woman I once knew. She was cool and clipped, which, all things considered, was the best possible outcome after what I'd done. There was no shaking the sense of walking to the gas chamber as I followed her down the hall to Magnus's study.

He stood in front of his desk, arms folded, looking me up and down, nodding toward one of the two chairs before him. "Thank you for your promptness," he gritted out as I approached. I had sat in that chair the day I first arrived in his home, recording our conversation for the sake of AI training. Looking back, I shuddered at my ignorance and unforgivable arrogance.

Evelyn sat beside me, angled in my direction with her hands folded in her lap. The way they both stared at me, silently judging, told me I was expected to lead off the conversation. "I'll tell you whatever you want to know," I offered. "That's the least I can do."

"Damn right, it's the least you can do." Lifting his brows, Magnus added, "Exactly what did you think would happen? Would anything change if you blew my family to pieces? Would your life have improved in any way?"

"Of course not," I murmured as I forced myself to hold his gaze. Nothing he said could top what I'd told myself for a solid week.

"I understand you had it rough, I'll give you that," he grumbled. "Leila for a mother. A father you never knew."

"How do you know I never knew him?"

"I know a lot about you, or haven't you figured that out yet?" Now, I sat before the real Magnus Miller. Gone was the warm, almost overly welcoming father figure. "Your father was some nobody from Brooklyn who dropped your mother the second he found out she was pregnant. Sabrina Duncan told me so. You met her at the gala. I saw the two of you chatting and tracked her down after you left. She set me straight on a lot of things, and I went about confirming what I could. The only thing I can't confirm so easily is your mother's motives, though I have no trouble believing she'd be so mercenary."

His smirk sent a chill down my spine. "What a shame Sabrina couldn't have introduced you to the true Leila before you took advantage of my family's kindness and broke my daughter's heart. For what it's worth, I would never have rejected you. If only your mother had given me a chance."

My soul shriveled beneath the weight of his judgment and the justifiable rage simmering just beneath the surface of his words. It revealed itself in the tightening of his jaw, the way every word felt forced.

"And that flunky of yours," he continued, teeth gritted. "That was some performance you two put on for everybody's sake. The little fight that landed him in the hospital. Does Aria know it was an act? Do any of them?"

When all I could do was gape at him, shocked, he released a derisive snort. "You honestly thought you were going to stroll in and pull the wool over my eyes? Like I'm some rube? I can see how it was so easy for your mother to get you twisted up."

"Magnus..." Evelyn murmured while I regretted breathing.

He knew.

He had always known.

Magnus ignored her. "It was your meeting at that shitty little diner that brought everything together. Did you think doing business in a different borough would throw me off your scent? You're an amateur."

There was nothing I could say and no defense I could

mount. I could only sit and take it, looking back through every step, every foolish mistake.

"Here's what I want to know." Unfolding his arms, he gripped the desk to either side of his body, his gaze unwavering. "Here you are. You made something of yourself despite everything life handed you from day one. No father, a mother who was absent more than she was present. You managed to avoid the pitfalls she dropped into. And there's nothing but a bright future out there for you. Why in the hell would you waste that for the sake of settling a score that wasn't yours to settle?"

I couldn't take any more. I would've rather he hit me than withstand this verbal onslaught. It was more than the words. It was the truth behind them. A truth that crushed me to the point where I bent forward, holding my head in my hands as the two of them watched. "I don't know anymore," I admitted. "I told myself to do it for her. I had blinders on. I couldn't see anything else."

"But why, dammit?" he growled out when Evelyn remained silent. "You were here. You lived with us. We took you in, we made you part of our family. How could you look us all in the face, knowing what you planned?"

"Have you ever had something drilled into your skull so many times, for so many years, that it becomes part of who you are?" I lifted my head from my hands, looking up at the man I was so sure had destroyed my chance at a normal life. It had never occurred to me to remember I'd built a damn good life despite everything.

"What are you talking about?" he asked, that cold gaze weighing on me.

"*All my life.* For as long as I can remember, she fed me the stories. I know, it's easy to blame her now that she's gone," I pointed out when his eyes narrowed. "That doesn't negate the truth. Everything that ever went wrong was your fault. She led me to believe you knew about me all along and didn't want to be a father. That you abandoned us for Evelyn. You humiliated her. You left her with nothing... no friends, no reputation, and certainly no money. The nights I spent hungry and alone were your fault, not hers. Hell, it never even occurred to me she wasn't working. She was partying, for fuck's sake."

I barked out a laugh at my own stupidity. How could I have continued believing her all these years? "Can't you understand? I promised to make you pay for something she fabricated. After a lifetime of feeling like I was the reason she couldn't make you stay with her, that I was the reason she ended up with nothing. Succeeding in spite of everything, punishing you, it became my reason for living. Everything she told me became the only truth I knew, and every step I took resulted from it. Can you imagine what that's like?"

"I don't have to imagine." It wasn't Magnus who spoke. It was Evelyn, still sitting in the chair beside me.

I lifted my head, looking at her in confusion. "What do you mean?"

She turned away from me, looking up at her husband. "When you think about it, it was the same for me," she murmured. "Every day of my life, someone told me how worthless and ugly and stupid I was. Over time, I believed I deserved to be hurt. You remember how I was when we first met and how long it took to undo all that damage."

She released a long breath, looking down at her folded hands. "And still, I have my moments."

Magnus groaned, his head tipping back until he looked up at the ceiling. "Fuck." That single word contained an entire volume.

"It's the truth," she pointed out in a soft voice. "And we both know what Leila was capable of. Nothing he's saying comes as any surprise to me."

"That's the thing," he muttered darkly. "I'm not surprised either. Why not use her own son to get back at me for something she did to herself thirty years ago?"

"I swear to you, I didn't know," I insisted. "Not until the night of the gala. I wanted to take back the envelope, truly," I told Evelyn, turning to her, silently pleading for her to understand. "But it was too late. You had already picked it up. I wish I could take it all back."

"I believe you," she whispered, nodding.

Something inside me broke at the sound of those three words. "Thank you," I whispered. "I am sorry. Truly, deeply sorry."

"That doesn't change a damn thing," Magnus reminded me. "You're lucky I haven't gone to the authorities yet. I have in my possession a device containing fabricated audio files compiled using recordings I did not consent to. I assume that's how you did it, right?"

I nodded, my heart sinking. This was it. I knew it was coming. "Are you going to the authorities with this?" I asked, miserable but knowing I deserved it.

"Don't have to," he decided. "All I have to do is talk to my good friend, Connor Diamond, and the world will know the lengths you're willing to go to. Even if it means manipulation, hacking, and manufacturing false records. Your name won't be worth shit a week from today."

By the time he finished, he sounded downright gleeful. "Once the dust settles, your company won't be worth shit either. Which is when I will purchase it, dismantle it, sell it for scrap."

Everything I had worked for. All of it, up in smoke. I

looked forward to a future now devoid of meaning, hope, and purpose.

I felt nothing. In the end, what did it matter?

"Do what you have to." I looked him in the eye again so he would know I meant it. "I won't stop you."

His head snapped back before he smirked. "Am I supposed to have a change of heart?"

"Not at all. I mean it. Do what you need to do, whatever you feel is necessary." Sitting back in the chair, I shrugged weakly. "I owe you that much, at least. I can never make up for the trust I broke. Or for the heart I broke, which you referred to earlier. The least I deserve is to lose everything I built because you're right. I lost sight of it. I don't deserve it."

Evelyn made a strained, strangled sound, staring up at her husband. I watched her from the corner of my eye while waiting for his reaction. It took time for his blank expression to shift to skepticism. "This is a trick."

"Try me," I invited. "See if I offer a fight. Do what needs to be done for all of you. Especially for Aria." Speaking her name was torture. It brought her precious face to the forefront of my mind. A face filled with pain and disbelief, thanks to me.

"Very well." Magnus shrugged at Evelyn before pushing away from the desk. "Don't say I didn't warn you."

"Wait!"

At first, I was sure I had to be imagining her voice. *Aria*. My bruised heart leaped at the sound, and I turned in my chair, stunned to find her rushing into the room and headed my way. "Wait, Dad. Hear me out."

"I thought you left," he muttered while Evelyn gasped, standing.

Aria came to a stop beside me. She wore workout

clothes not unlike what I'd first seen her in, though she'd clearly lost a bit of weight.

Because of me? Fuck.

Without meeting my gaze, she faced her father. "You can't hurt him, Dad."

Snorting, he asked, "Why not?"

"Because you would only end up hurting me too." At long last, she looked at me, and I could breathe again. How had I existed this past week without her? "Because I love him."

21

ARIA

Well, I didn't mean to blurt it out like that. Now that I had, there was no taking it back.

I didn't usually believe in fate or anything of the sort, but there had to be a reason why I had forgotten to pack the toiletries in my bathroom vanity this morning. I was sort of in a hurry at the time, and it was either sneak back in and duck out before anybody caught me or ordering a whole new set of skin care products. I didn't feel like going through the hassle.

I'd heard Dad almost shouting, but that wasn't what kept me from hurrying back out with my bag full of creams and serums. It was hearing Miles's voice raised in reply that made me creep up on the room and hide outside to listen.

He was willing to give up everything for me. I believed it. Nobody sounded as completely destroyed as he had when they didn't mean it.

Not only that, I'd heard what he said about his mom. What she did to him. Between that and what Dad had told me, I knew all I needed to know.

It was pretty obvious my parents weren't as convinced.

"Aria, sweetheart..." Mom murmured, glancing between Dad and me. "Are you sure about this?"

"I know what I'm saying." Turning to Dad, I nodded, making him wince. "Like I said, you could have warned me. You didn't, and this is what happened. I'm not sorry it did. Not anymore."

Miles hadn't looked away from me since I came into the room. His mouth was partly open, and his eyes were narrowed like he wasn't sure he could believe what he heard.

"I can't approve of this." Dad shook his head fiercely when Mom tried to stop him from being an ass and saying something stupid. "It would be one thing to ask me not to grind him into dust after what he did because he had his reasons. But because you love him? After everything he did, you can tell me that?"

"Yes. I can." I squeezed Miles's shoulder. "He was going to tell me what he did when you found us at the gala. He said something about making a mistake, but that was all he got out. He could've run away, but he stayed because he wanted to try to make it right with me somehow before it was too late. I understand that now. I understand a lot more than I did before."

Mom offered a tiny smile, which gave me hope. "What about you, Miles?" she asked him.

Dad cut Miles off with the slash of his hand through the air. "Enough. Like he wouldn't say whatever it took to save his ass. I will not allow my daughter to be used like that. Not again."

"I don't blame you." Miles stood, facing Dad head-on. When I first rounded the doorway, he looked defeated. Now, he stood straight and tall, and the new strength in his voice made my chest swell. "I would think the same way if I were in your shoes. I haven't given you any reason to trust me until now. The best I can say is I will work every day to earn your trust. All of you. Though I know I don't deserve your daughter, I do love her. I would've realized it sooner and been able to do something about it if I hadn't been so damn blind. I see what's important now."

"Nice words," Dad muttered sarcastically, making me grind my teeth rather than scream at him to listen. "Anyone can throw words around."

"What about actions?" Miles countered.

"Meaning?"

"Meaning I have my legal team in the process of drawing up paperwork to form a nonprofit foundation focused on kids from poor neighborhoods, with backgrounds like mine."

That was news to me, but then it would be after a week of no contact. "I have to do something to help them," he explained. "Seeing them at that carnival…"

He turned to Mom. "There was a boy who reminded me much too much of myself at his age. I could've used a community around me in those days. Mentors, guidance. Hell, free food after school and help with my homework. I want to provide that now. You help the moms. I'll help the kids."

Mom's eyes lit up. "We could work together," she concluded with a smile.

"Wait a second." Dad was still having none of it, and it took everything I had not to stomp my feet like a spoiled kid. Why was he so damn impossible? "Now we're talking about working with him?"

"Give him a chance," I whispered. "Dad, please."

He pushed away from the desk, ignoring Mom when she reached for him. We exchanged a worried look as he rounded the desk, standing with his back to us and gazing out the window. Miles reached up and took my hand from his shoulder, lacing his fingers with mine. It felt so right. I was so proud of him.

Still, a part of me would always be filled with regret if Dad never came around and accepted us.

Dad's shoulders rose and fell. "Clearly, I'm outnumbered," he admitted with a sigh. "Don't expect me to be thrilled about this. I do believe you have decent intentions, Miles. Don't make me regret not picking up that phone and calling Connor."

"I promise I won't." His grip on my hand tightened. "You know I keep my promises."

Dad snickered, turning his head and smirking over his shoulder. "You've proven that much. And, Pumpkin?" His gaze softened along with his voice. "I love you."

My throat tightened, but I managed to croak, "I love you, Dad."

Mom came over, gently shooing us out of the room. "Go ahead. Give him some time." She kissed my cheek, ushering us across the threshold, then closed the door, leaving us alone in the hall.

We had been here before—moments after leaving Dad's study that first day, face-to-face. Now, I wasn't filled with apprehension and mistrust. Not like before. Never again.

"Are you sure about this?" It was like he was afraid to touch me as he gently brushed his fingers over my cheek, stroking my hair behind my ear. That simple touch drained the strength from me. All I wanted was to lean in, to melt into his arms. Thank God I came back when I had. I would never stop being grateful for a simple twist of fate.

"Absolutely sure," I told him with a smile and a heart

ready to burst. "I heard everything you said. And I'm sorry you had to—"

He shook his head, then touched his forehead to mine, releasing a sigh. "Enough of my past. It's time to start thinking about the future."

"The immediate future or long-term?" I was ready to explode with joy by the time I opened my eyes to look deep into his. Was this real? Had my dreams come true all at once? It certainly felt that way. "Because in the immediate future, I would like very much to be alone with you."

His full mouth stirred in the beginnings of a knowing grin. "I think that can be arranged."

~

"Oh, God! Yes!" I held Miles's head in place, grinding against his face, riding the waves of pleasure brought on by his tongue against my clit. He was a master, working my body like an instrument. I was made for him, and he was made for me.

Instead of letting up, he drove his tongue inside me, fucking me with it and teasing my clit with his thumb. Fireworks burst behind my closed eyelids, red, gold, and silver, my core clenching again before the sweetest spasms wracked me from head to toe. Fuck, he was good at that.

He was good at a lot of things, like stretching out on his back and pulling me on top of him without any effort. We didn't need to talk through it. I knew what he needed because I needed it too.

We both went still when I took him inside me, savoring that first moment of penetration as I sank to his base. "There is nothing like being inside you," he whispered, running his hands up my thighs as I began to move. "So tight. So wet."

"Let me feel every inch of you," I groaned out, rolling my hips when I reached his base, moaning at the pressure against my G-spot. Sheer torture and I wouldn't have given up a second of it.

I was so sure we would never be here again.

"Miles... Miles..." Right away, the tension began building again. Maybe I had never stopped coming after the last one. All I knew was my body plunged up and down on top of his, riding him hard and fast. He was back where he belonged, inside me. Connected.

"God, I love you," he whispered, touching me, stroking, lighting me on fire. Flames licked my skin, or was that his tongue when he sat up, pulling me close, burying his face in my neck, and groaning when I picked up speed? Close, so close.

"I love you," I whispered in his ear, my fingers dancing in his hair, my breath coming in sharp gasps. That was all I knew. I loved him. I loved this. His heart racing against mine, his hands tugging my hair, pulling my head back so his tongue could trace the line of my throat.

It was more now. The mind-bending heat hadn't changed. It was everything else. How precious he was to me. How close I came to losing him forever. The thought made me wrap my arms around his shoulders so I could hold him tight like I was afraid he would get away from me again.

"Are you ready to come for me?" he growled out, his breath hot against my skin.

"Yes... yes!" So ready that it scared me. I was almost afraid of the force building in my core. Tears filled my eyes, and emotion clogged my throat. I held him tighter because I knew I would be safe. "Come with me." I nearly sobbed.

The tension grew until there was nothing to do but scream when it all exploded, shattering me. My body clenched around him when he poured himself into me. When he fell back, I went with him, draped across his chest, completely spent after our third round of earth-shattering sex since arriving at The Plaza that afternoon.

"I think I'm going to need a break now," he panted beneath me. "And maybe a little food. We missed dinner."

"No wonder I'm so hungry." It didn't help that I hadn't eaten a decent meal in days. It's funny how all of a sudden, my appetite was back with a vengeance.

But it was so much nicer right now to be here, like this. Forgetting the outside world existed, if only for a little while. Later, there would be time to make explanations to answer texts and phone calls from everybody once they heard what happened. By now, I had no doubt the news had spread. Mom would have called my sister immediately, and after that, it was only a matter of a group text.

I'd deal with it later. Not now. Not yet.

"Thank you," he whispered softly enough that I almost didn't hear him over my pounding heart.

I opened my eyes and lifted my head, looking down at him. Those beautiful eyes were even more beautiful now that they were filled with love. So much so that I could barely breathe. "For what?" I whispered, brushing a few damp curls away from his forehead.

"For this. Giving me another chance. I know I don't deserve it."

I touched a finger to his lips, shaking my head. "Like you said, let's not talk about the past anymore. All that matters is now."

He took my hand, pressing his lips to my palm and

closing his eyes. "I don't know what I did to deserve you, but I'm going to work every day to keep you happy."

I rolled away, giggling as I reached for the room service menu on the nightstand. "You can start by ordering a feast to be sent up here. After that, we'll take it one day at a time."

"Everything in life should be so easy," he replied, snatching the menu from me.

He made a point. Loving him was so easy. I had started doing it before I knew what was happening.

It's a good thing, since I planned to do it for the rest of my life.

EPILOGUE
VALENTINA

"You know I'm going to help you plan this wedding, right?" Taking Rose's hand in mine, I lifted it to admire her dazzling ring for the hundredth time since I arrived at her loft apartment. The engagement party was in full swing, with people laughing, drinking, and congratulating the happy couple.

Rose was radiant, absolutely glowing as she accepted congratulations from a passing guest before turning back to me. "You know I would love to be hands-on," she confessed with a nervous giggle. "The store has me so busy and everything. I want it to be perfect."

"It will be," I promised, gazing at the princess-cut diamond one more time and letting her go. "You know I've got you."

Sienna grabbed her from behind, arms around her waist. "I can't believe you're going to be my sister!" she squealed.

"Hey, don't hog the bride-to-be." Colton sauntered over, a drink in hand, smiling just as wide and as brightly as his fiancée.

Sienna stuck her tongue out at him. "You get her for the rest of your life, brother," she reminded him as I laughed. "I can hug her every once in a while."

"There's more than enough of me to go around," Rose reminded them both, and the four of us cracked up before Colton led Rose away to talk to more of their guests. We couldn't take up all of their time.

Things were changing. We weren't kids anymore. Some of us were ready to move into new phases of their lives. I caught Sienna giving Noah a meaningful look from across the room while nearby, my sister canoodled with Miles Young, our stepbrother, and her new boyfriend. People were pairing off, planning futures. That was a good thing. No matter how empty it left me feeling inside.

Evan and Lucian wandered over, and I eyed them both suspiciously. "What, you can't find some willing girl to chat up?" I teased, waving a hand to indicate the many such girls around us. Rose had modeled for her family's couture line during college and still had a lot of friends from those days.

"These girls?" Evan snickered, shaking his head. "Been there."

"All of them?" I asked, skeptical. The guys got around. That was no secret. But even for him, it seemed like a lot.

Lucian burst out laughing. "Please, like he could remember all their faces. More like every woman here has marriage on the brain. Picking up pussy at an engagement party is a dangerous move."

I could see the truth in that, so I didn't offer a reply, settling for sipping my wine when a high-pitched whistle from the far end of the living room caught my attention. The room went quieter before Colton spoke. "Rose and I want to thank you for joining us here tonight. It means everything to us that we get to celebrate this event with all of you."

He exchanged a glance with Rose, who nodded, then he continued, "There's another event we'd like to share with you now. It seems like we couldn't stop at planning a wedding. We are also building our new family, as I speak. Rather, Rose is."

It took a second for understanding to sink in. That glow of hers wasn't all because of the engagement.

"We're having a baby." Colton barely got the sentence out before the room erupted in a chorus of squeals, cheers, and applause. It was a wave of sound and emotion that threatened to drown the two of them as they were quickly surrounded by well-wishers.

My feet wouldn't move. I couldn't muster a smile.

Not when I looked past Lucian to where Evan stood, his gaze lingering on me.

That was all it took to bring the past rushing back.

Our past.

READ VALENTINA'S STORY NEXT…

Delicious Tropes you can expect:
Second chance, Forced Proximity, Friends to Lovers, Tragic Past & Hidden Desires

Preorder SILENT CRAVINGS today!

BONUS SCENE

Don't want to let Miles and Aria go just yet?

Grab the FREE bonus scene here:

https://dl.bookfunnel.com/7rj86t1iih

ALSO BY MISSY WALKER

ELITE HEIRS OF MANHATTAN SERIES

Seductive Hearts

Sweet Surrender

Sinful Desires

Silent Cravings

Sensual Games

ELITE MEN OF MANHATTAN SERIES

Forbidden Lust*

Forbidden Love*

Lost Love

Missing Love

Guarded Love

Infinite Love Novella

ELITE MAFIA OF NEW YORK SERIES

Cruel Lust*

Stolen Love

Finding Love

SLATER SIBLINGS SERIES

Hungry Heart

Chained Heart

Iron Heart

Small town desires series

Trusting the Rockstar

Trusting the Ex

Trusting the Player

*Forbidden Lust/Love are a duet and to be read in order.

*Cruel Lust is a trilogy and to be read in order

All other books are stand alones.

JOIN MISSY'S BOOK BABES

Hear about exclusive book releases, teasers, discounts and book bundles before anyone else.

Sign up to Missy's newsletter here:
www.authormissywalker.com

Become part of Missy's Facebook Reader Group where we chat all things books, releases and of course fun giveaways!

https://www.facebook.com/groups/missywalkersbookbabes

ACKNOWLEDGMENTS

This was my first time writing a stepbrother trope, and I thoroughly enjoyed the experience. I hope that joy comes through in my writing and that you were reading those pages with gusto! I'm already feeling the itch to write another one soon! :)

A special thanks to my editors, Chantell, Kay, and Nicki. Your feedback was invaluable. To my wonderful betas, Ella, Karmin, Maria, and Saskia, your patience and support were essential in getting this story just right.

I want to express my gratitude to all my fans, especially to my Facebook reader group, Missy Walker's Book Babes! Building this community online has been incredible, and I love reading everything you all post.

We all need an escape, and that's what I aim to provide with each book I create. Life can be challenging, and my hope is that my books offer a little light when it's needed and that our reader community can be there for each other.

With much love,
    Missy x

ABOUT THE AUTHOR

Missy is an Australian author who writes kissing books with equal parts angst and steam. Stories about billionaires, forbidden romance, and second chances roll around in her mind probably more than they ought to.

When she's not writing, she's taking care of her two daughters and doting husband and conjuring up her next saucy plot.

Inspired by the acreage she lives on, Missy regularly distracts herself by visiting her orchard, baking naughty but delicious foods, and socialising with her girl squad.

Then there's her overweight cat—Charlie, chickens, and border collie dog—Benji if she needed another excuse to pass the time.

If you like Missy Walker's books, consider leaving a review and following her here:

>   instagram.com/missywalkerauthor
>   facebook.com/AuthorMissyWalker
>   tiktok.com/@authormissywalker
>   bookbub.com/profile/missy-walker

Printed in Great Britain
by Amazon